Stay Wicked!
Sawyer Bennett

Wicked Choice

(The Wicked Horse Vegas Series)

By
Sawyer Bennett

All Rights Reserved.

Copyright © 2017 by Sawyer Bennett

Published by Big Dog Books

This book is a work of fiction. Names, characters, places, and incidents either are products of the author's imagination or are used fictitiously. Any resemblance to actual events, locales or persons, living or dead, is entirely coincidental.

No part of this book can be reproduced in any form or by electronic or mechanical means including information storage and retrieval systems, without the express written permission of the author. The only exception is by a reviewer who may quote short excerpts in a review.

ISBN: 978-1-940883-98-4

Since the release of her debut contemporary romance novel, Off Sides, in January 2013, Sawyer Bennett has released multiple books, many of which have appeared on the New York Times, USA Today and Wall Street Journal bestseller lists.

Find Sawyer on the web!
sawyerbennett.com
twitter.com/bennettbooks
facebook.com/bennettbooks

Table of Contents

Foreword v
PROLOGUE 1
CHAPTER 1 11
CHAPTER 2 21
CHAPTER 3 30
CHAPTER 4 42
CHAPTER 5 52
CHAPTER 6 63
CHAPTER 7 74
CHAPTER 8 85
CHAPTER 9 96
CHAPTER 10 106
CHAPTER 11 117
CHAPTER 12 128
CHAPTER 13 138
CHAPTER 14 149
CHAPTER 15 163
CHAPTER 16 176
CHAPTER 17 186
CHAPTER 18 196
CHAPTER 19 209
CHAPTER 20 220

CHAPTER 21	230
CHAPTER 22	239
CHAPTER 23	248
CHAPTER 24	257
EPILOGUE	267
Connect with Sawyer online:	276
About the Author	277

Foreword

Dear Reader:

If you're a Wicked Horse Vegas veteran, then you'll notice this book is a little different than the previous ones. That's because Wicked Choice is actually a bridge book—meaning it's going to spin off into an exciting new series. I can't tell you a lot of details yet because the spin-off is going to happen as part of an amazing collaboration with another author. What I can tell you is that the new series will focus on The Jameson Group. It will still be as sexy as The Wicked Horse series, but it will have a bit of a suspense element to it. The first book is scheduled to launch in early 2019. Stay tuned.

One other thing…

I tend to cap my series at five books, but I've decided to keep The Wicked Horse Vegas alive. I anticipate releasing at least two a year for the foreseeable future, or until my readers are no longer interested in what happens inside of Vegas' hottest sex club.

Love,
Sawyer

PROLOGUE

Rachel

THE BANGING ON my hotel door takes a moment to penetrate. I'm not sure if it's because I'm four shots of bourbon past the pleasantly buzzed state, or because I'm sick with exhaustion and guilt.

After stepping out of the shower, I ignore my dripping hair and wrap a fluffy white towel around my body. I attempt to ignore the shallow wound on my upper right arm, but it's throbbing mercilessly and the bourbon's not helping.

The banging continues, and I yell grumpily as I make my way across the spacious luxury hotel room, "Hold your fucking horses, Wright."

Immediately, the pounding stops, but I knew it would. Bodie Wright is the only person who knows this is my room, and I left strict instructions with the front desk I wasn't to be disturbed for anything.

I unlock the door and swing it open so fast I take a stumbling step back. I normally hold my liquor much better, but I'm going on twenty-four hours without food and more than that without sleep.

"What?" I snarl as he steps into my room, towering over my five-eight frame by a good half a foot or so. I can tell he's had a shower because he smells good and his short, dark hair is wet.

Bodie's eyes immediately drop to my arm and they harden as he takes in the barely two-inch groove caused by a bullet that grazed me.

"It's fine," I mumble.

"Figures," he replies dryly as he walks over to my patrol pack I'd thrown to the floor a few hours ago when we checked in. With casual ease, he retrieves the IFAK—individual first aid kit—and pulls out some gauze and tape. This is the second time Bodie has treated my wound—the first time was while we sped away on a Syrian boat down the coast to Tripoli. The IFAK can treat anything from a shallow bullet trench to a sucking chest wound. He'd used most of our QuikClot combat gauze to stop the hemorrhaging in our teammate Joram's bullet hole just below his collarbone, but there was enough left that he could slap a quick covering on my arm to curb the bleeding.

It wasn't the first time I'd been shot at, but it was the first time that a bullet had hit me and I didn't even feel any pain. I was so amped on adrenaline and fear because of Joram's wound that I hadn't even known I'd been hit, until Bodie started working on me in the boat after he got Joram as stabilized as he could be given the circumstances.

We made landing just north of Tripoli at a prearranged extraction point. From there, Stan, our pilot, flew us to Cypress on an MV22 Osprey that Kynan somehow managed to procure through CIA contacts and favors owed.

"Sit down and let me wrap that," Bodie orders.

Despite the fact he's younger than I am by almost nine years—and he's only been with Jameson Group a few years—his tone says he's not to be trifled with right now.

I'm too inebriated to argue. Plus… I've got to give the dude props. When we got ambushed, he handled our extraction like a seasoned pro, carrying Joram to the boat while bullets flew.

I walk toward the bed, but take a side trip to the wet bar where I grab the bottle of bourbon and ignore the glass I'd been using. In Cypress, most would think I'd be taking advantage of their ouzo, but I hate the taste of licorice. Instead, I went with a tried and true favorite of mine.

When my butt hits the edge of the bed, I twist the cap off and take a healthy slug. I hand it toward Bodie as he lays out the medical supplies, but he shakes his head.

Goody two-shoes.

It doesn't bother me that I'm half naked in front of Bodie. When we're on a mission, my teammates don't look at me like a woman. They don't care what I look like or that I have periods.

I've spent weeks with my male teammates, and we've all seen each other naked at one time or another. There's no time for sensibilities while on a mission. Not to mention, we've all spent time at The Wicked Horse. While it's sort of an unwritten rule, or at least an understanding, that we don't mix in *that* way, many of us do hang out at the sex club quite regularly. I'm sure Bodie has watched me in action.

But all he cares about is that I can do my job, and therein lies the guilt that's consuming me.

I got Joram shot.

"The wound looks clean, and it's not seeping anymore," Bodie says as he gently takes my arm to peer at it. I look down, fascinated by the groove in my flesh and the whitish-pink wet skin underneath.

I take another swig of the bourbon and Bodie goes to work, dabbing on some antibiotic-laced ointment and wrapping a dry gauze around my upper arm. He efficiently secures the ends with tape and pronounces me cured.

I can't even muster up a grateful smile. Instead, I tip the bottle back to my mouth. To my surprise, Bodie takes the bottle from me and mutters, "You need to slow down."

"Fuck you," I snarl as I push up from the bed, swaying only slightly, and hold my hand out for the bottle.

Bodie's dark eyes scrutinize me and I feel like a bug under a magnifying glass. He hasn't shaved for days, and that scruff makes him look older and wiser than his twenty-six years.

I snap my fingers, indicating to pass the booze, and he finally gives a sigh. Turning to the wet bar, he pours two glasses halfway to the rim with the amber liquid. Setting the bottle down, he picks the glasses up and hands me one.

I take it from him, trying to ignore the way my head swims from the bourbon, lack of food, and sleep. I still have enough sense within me to slow it down a bit, and I take a delicate sip.

Bodie moves a few steps back and plops down in one of the cushy armchairs. The hotel Kynan arranged for us is five-star with no amenity lacking. It's not a reward for a job well done, but rather he thinks it looks less suspicious for us to pretend to be vacationers. So, we're going to spend two nights here in Paphos, Cypress before we head back to the States, and I intend to use the time catching up on my sleep.

If I can sleep, that is.

Thus, the reason for the bourbon.

"It's not your fault," Bodie says quietly, and I come to a dead stop. It's then I realize I'd been pacing, and my agitation was loud and clear.

As is my guilt, apparently.

"My perimeter was bad," I say in a pissy voice.

His eyes go hot with anger. "Your perimeter was fine given what we were working with," he practically snarls as he comes out of his chair, bourbon swishing over the edge of his glass. "The munitions dump was thirty clicks west of where the intel said it was. We did the best we could with what we had."

Bodie comes at me like a cat, and I know without a doubt I'd never want him stalking me as a potential kill. He's one of our explosives' guys, so his job was to rig and detonate a known ISIS munitions dump, but he's still got wicked skills when it comes to hand-to-hand combat. Four years in the Navy SEALs hones all the broad-based skills needed as a mercenary.

Coming to a stop before me, Bodie bends down so his face hovers over mine. "We had limited intel, and we gambled to go forward with what we had."

"I made the decision to go forward," I say bitterly. I turn away from him and walk toward the bed. I'm the team leader, and it was my call to finish the mission without complete knowledge of what we were facing.

I bring the glass to my mouth and take a long swallow, hissing through my teeth.

"Put the booze down, Hart," Bodie says tauntingly, calling me by my last name, which is how we usually address each other on assignment. "It's making you morose."

I know deep down he's doing what any team member would do, and that's to get me to suck it up. It's not the first mission that didn't go perfectly, and it won't be the last. But I think of Joram, our guide and interpreter, who is in surgery right now because he took a bullet high in his chest, and I flush with self-directed anger.

Hot, irrational fury rages through me, and I decide to take it out on my teammate.

"Fuck you, Bodie," I yell as I turn on him, cocking my good arm back. I let the glass fly at his head, but his reflexes are too good. He just ducks slightly to the side and it sails past, smashing against the far wall. Good bourbon goes spraying everywhere.

And it pisses me off even more that he's right and I'm wrong. That he easily ducked my glass when I would have probably felt better if it hit him in the face. And mostly because he's standing there looking at me with sympathy when that's not what I want or need.

"Fuck you," I yell again as I take long, angry strides at him. He watches me warily, body fully tense as if he's playing chicken with a freight train that's barreling at him.

All of my anger and guilt goes on a nuclear boil, and I wonder at this moment if Joram's family hates me for the role I placed him in and the danger that got him shot.

"Fuck you," I yell again as my hands slam into his chest.

Bodie has about seventy pounds on me, but he doesn't budge an inch. It causes me to see red, since it's a subtle reminder that I am, after all, just a girl playing at a man's game. I lean back, pull my arms in to launch another strike, but before I can try to push him again, his large hands come down on my shoulders.

"You need to dial it down, Rachel," he tells me in a deceptively calm voice.

I want to scratch his eyes out and knee him in the nuts for being so fucking right, but I forcibly try to release my anger instead.

But it's bottled tight when I remember the sound of the bullet as it hit Joram—a whizzing, thudding combo with a wet smack—and his grunt of pain before he sagged to the ground beside me. Bodie didn't see it because he was busy detonating his charges, and I didn't make a sound when the bullet destined for me tore through the flesh of my upper arm.

Rage and guilt and booze swim through my blood. For a split second, I feel like I'm in another world. But then my eyes focus and I see Bodie staring down at me, his eyes soft and almost nurturing, and I hate that even more.

"Fuck you," I curse under my breath right before I choose to get my release another way.

I jump on him.

That gets the big lug to move since he's so surprised by my attack. But it's not to hit him or strike out in my anger. It's a way to release my emotions in a way that feels good.

My legs spread and go around his hips, locking tight. Hands to his neck, I stare at him for what seems like an eternity but is only a second or two, and then my mouth is on his.

Bodie makes an unholy sound from deep within his chest. For a moment, I think it's disgust, but then his hands go from my shoulders down to my naked ass, bare since the towel fell away from my body.

We kiss so hard my lips feel bruised and my blood now rages with something other than anger.

Pure white-hot lust.

Digging his fingers into my flesh, Bodie mutters something foul, or perhaps it's beautiful, into my mouth, but I really don't care. He spins us around and takes me to the mattress, knocking the breath out of me as his big body pins me down.

My hands slither in between us, working at the belt to his pants. When my knuckles graze against an impressively big erection, I know I'm embarrassingly wet for him right now.

Bodie pulls his mouth from mine and looks down at me, his eyes almost black as pitch. "What are we doing, Hart?"

If I thought his use of my professional team name would quell my raging lust, I'd be totally wrong. It means nothing to me that he's even questioning this.

"We're getting ready to fuck," I pant desperately before leaning up to nip at his lower lip with my teeth.

He curses again, and then his hands are on me.

All over me.

In me.

And I forget about Joram for just a little bit.

CHAPTER 1

Bodie

6 weeks later...

"I'M OUT," I mutter as I fold my cards and lay them face down on the green felt poker table. Tonight's just not my night.

Pushing out of my chair, I ignore Kynan's snicker as he's been taking most of our money all night.

I make my way over to the bar being staffed by two drop-dead gorgeous waitresses. The blonde I have carnal knowledge of, but the brunette is more to my taste. I wonder if they'd be up for a three-way with me.

I hadn't intended to get laid tonight when I came to The Wicked Horse. Well, wait... who the fuck am I kidding? People don't come to The Wicked Horse without the probability of busting a nut, but it wasn't my primary motive.

No, tonight is about hanging with some of my team and unwinding. I just came off a mission to Riyadh where we provided extra security for a lower-ranked foreign diplomat. Not overly exciting but not all that dull either.

Still, I'm always exhausted after any mission that involves danger, and I suppose it's the constant hum of adrenaline that percolates every second of every day. The resulting let down after it's all done is draining.

I'm tight with everyone in the Jameson Group, but more so with the actual men and women I go on high-risk operations with. The bond is deeper, forged in trust and a mutual need to keep each other safe. When we get back to the States, we usually hit up a bar, hang out at someone's house for a cookout, or chill playing poker in the private club simply known as "The Apartment" at The Wicked Horse. The Apartment is a nod to Jerico Jameson, the founder and former owner of The Jameson Group, since he used to live here full time after he opened The Wicked Horse. Now he's committed himself to a woman and they live in Vegas suburbia, so this space got converted to a private club within a sex club. Here is mostly where people drink and chat—with all the fucking going on in the other rooms at The Wicked Horse. Doesn't mean fucking doesn't go on in here, but it doesn't happen a lot. There are too many other fun places to get your rocks off within the entirety of the club.

The brunette bartender leans over the counter and places her forearms there for support. This gives me a fantastic display of cleavage spilling out over a black bustier she's wearing. "What can I get you?"

"Budweiser," I say, and her eyebrows dart upward.

To be a member of this private club means having money out the wazoo, and I am indeed quite well off because of the work I do. I'm sure there aren't many private club members that drink domestic, but the great thing about paying loads of money to be a member of the private club means they stock my favorite brew.

"Not a very fancy beer," she says, leaning to reach into a cooler. She pulls out a bottle and pops the top for me.

"Not a very fancy man," I tell her as I accept it. I'm a Nebraska farm boy who has been drinking Bud since I was fourteen. Can't help it if that's still my thing. In fact, it reminds me of warm summer nights and getting drunk down at the rock quarry while my friends and I swam naked and fucked around with the prettiest cheerleaders available.

"Hey, Bodie," the blonde says as she comes to stand near the brunette. "Anything on tap for tonight?"

"Not yet," I tell her with a grin. "You offering?"

The blonde and brunette share a look, and I know my idea of a three-way isn't mine alone.

"We get off in about an hour," the blonde says. "Want to play in The Silo with us?"

Fuck yes, I want to play with them in The Silo. It's my favorite room at The Wicked Horse, mainly because of the variety of gadgets and machines up for use in there. Being with two women is a tricky business. To make sure they're both satisfied, there's an industrial dildo in there just waiting to hammer some pussy. My dick starts to get hard thinking about it.

"See you there in about an hour then," I tell the ladies with a nod.

"Looking forward to it," the brunette says.

Oh, me too.

I turn away from the bar, content to just stand and watch my buddies continue the poker game. Kynan McGrath owns The Jameson Group now, and he led our operation in Riyadh. Including me, we have three other men who make up Eagle Team One.

Eagle is the name of our high-profile security group. I belong to Team One along with my best friend Cage Murdock, a wily southern boy from North Carolina. Our team is completed with Locke Meyers and August Greenfield, both former law enforcement turned security specialists. In addition to doing security on the Eagle team, I'm also on a Renegade team, which is our special-ops division.

As I walk back toward the poker table, I catch movement from the corner of my eye. My entire body tenses up when I see Rachel Hart walking toward me.

We've barely spoken ten words to each other since our mission in Paphos, and the reason for that is two-fold. First and foremost, I've been on Eagle operations since then, and Hart has been... well, elsewhere.

Secondarily, I think we're avoiding each other because what happened in that hotel in Paphos shouldn't have happened. Hart was nearly drunk, and we were both sapped of any common sense following such a harrowing mission. While members of The Jameson Group tend to hang out at The Wicked Horse since the founder of our company is the owner of this esteemed sex club, we never cross lines by fucking each other. It's not a written rule, but it's totally understood. We can't afford to have personal connections muddying up waters when we need to have crystal clarity in all situations.

Still, as Hart walks toward me, I can't help but remember that night because it was hot as fuck. Probably the best sex of my life. That's because she's gorgeous and adventurous in bed, but mostly because I respect her as a capable and trustworthy teammate.

It hits me all at once, though, that I don't think she's at The Wicked Horse to play. Oddly, that relieves me somewhat. It's not something I can tell from her expression alone. Many of the guys tease her, telling her she has "resting bitch face," but I've never thought that. In my mind, she wore a determined look because she's one of the most seriously determined people I know. She's got that look tonight, but that's par for the course.

Usually when she is on the prowl at the club, Hart would be wearing a dress barely covering her tits and ass, which never lets anyone forget that she's first and foremost all woman. I expect it's a nice change from sweaty combat gear and the stench of danger she normally wears.

Tonight, Hart is wearing a pair of faded jeans with rips in the knees, a V-neck shirt that fits her nicely but isn't overly sexy, and a pair of tennis shoes. Her nearly midnight-colored hair that normally sits just below her jawline is pulled into a stubby ponytail, and she's devoid of makeup. When she's playing in the club, she always wears dark eye makeup, which makes her pale blue eyes stand out so brightly it's hard to look away from them.

She doesn't even spare a glance at the poker table, but her eyes stay locked on mine. A feeling of immense apprehension takes root deep within me.

"Hart," Locke calls out, but I don't look away from her gaze. "Come play poker with us. Wright's too much of a pussy to continue."

She shoots a glance his way, gives a tight smile, and says, "Can't tonight."

And then, they're forgotten when she reaches me. With lips pressed into a grimace, she murmurs, "I need to talk to you. Privately."

"Okay," I say somewhat hesitantly, but I put my beer down at a nearby table, prepared to follow her wherever she wants to go for a private discussion.

Hart spins and marches out of The Apartment. I take in the set to her spine and the way her hands are clenched into fists. Same hands that were clenched around my cock six weeks ago—

Okay, stop that.

I follow her down the private hallway, through the Social Room, and into the private elevator that takes us to street level. It's slightly chilly outside. While the temps can get in the upper eighties in Vegas in mid-May, the evenings still call for a light jacket. Hart's hands come up and cross to rub at her bare arms. I can faintly see the pink scar left by the bullet.

I'm surprised when she does a quick look left and right down the street, and then darts across when there's an immediate break in traffic. I jog behind her, following her to an empty bus stop bench.

Hart takes a seat and I sit down as well, angling my body so I can face her.

She pulls no punches with me, but then, Hart isn't the type of woman to ever sugarcoat anything.

"I'm pregnant," she says bluntly. Since I'm the one she's telling this information to, I know it means I'm the one who knocked her up.

"Fuck," I mutter, dragging a hand through my short hair. I knew this was a possibility.

That night was all kinds of wild and crazy. Neither one of us had any condoms and in hindsight, neither of us cared. With Hart fisting my cock and rubbing the head through her wet folds, I was dizzy with fucking lust.

Her soft words, "Just pull out, okay," told me all I needed to know.

I was going to fuck Hart, and there was no stopping

that train.

She was safe or else she would have never said that to me. The trust I had in her was inherent as evidenced by the fact I let her cover my back while I blew up an ISIS camp. It also meant she trusted me, or else she knew I would have said no if I wasn't safe.

Her words also told me she wasn't on the Pill, and there was a risk of pregnancy.

Except there was no explaining that to my dick or her uterus, because I plunged in hard and deep. She responded by digging her nails into my back and drawing little half-moons of blood.

In my mind, I'd pulled out in perfect fashion. Jacked my cock three times and came all over her stomach and breasts. It was one of the hottest things I'd ever seen.

Guess something of me got left behind, though. I remember all about sex education in school, and I know damn well a woman can get pregnant even if the pull-out method is employed.

Apparently, being the risk takers that we were, it just didn't matter to us that night.

Still, a flush of guilt heats me up from within. Hart had been drinking, and she was emotionally vulnerable that night.

I should have fucking said no.

"You're sure?" I ask, not doubting it's mine, just curious if she's been tested.

She nods. "I didn't think anything of it when I

missed my period because I'm not regular, but I'd been having some nausea and my boobs started hurting. I took a home pregnancy test, and it was positive. Had Doc McCullough do a blood test, and he called me this afternoon to tell me it was positive."

"Jesus," I murmur as I give her my sincerest, most apologetic look. "I'm sorry, Rachel."

She flinches, and I know it's because of my tone and the fact I called her by her first name.

"I don't want a baby," she says flatly, her expression bordering on hopeless.

I've never even thought about this moment transpiring. I'm years from settling down, marrying, and having kids. But something instinctive rises within me, and I find myself blurting out, "I want it."

Hart blinks at me in surprise. "You want a baby?"

"If it's mine, and I believe you when you say it is, then yes... I want it."

Her eyes go dull, and her voice is practically listless. "Then let me rephrase. I don't want to carry a baby. I don't want to be pregnant."

"And I don't want you to end my child's life," I say softly, forcing myself to remain calm. "Because when you say you don't want to be pregnant or carry a baby, you're talking about getting an abortion, right?"

Hart grinds her teeth in agitation, but I can see the conflict in her eyes. "You seriously want me to carry a baby for you to raise? You think you can do that with the career you have?"

Again, I fly by pure instinct. "No. I couldn't continue in this line of work and raise a kid by myself. I'd probably move back home and work my parents' farm."

Hart's jaw drops, and she stares at me blankly.

"Rachel," I say pleadingly. "Please do not terminate the pregnancy. I know I'm asking an awful lot of you, but this is important to me. The most important thing that's ever been laid in my lap, and I can't tell you why I feel so strongly about this, but I just know that I do. It would kill me if you terminated something I'd created. That may sound dramatic, and you're really throwing me here, but I have an obligation to this child. If you don't want a part in raising it, I get it. But don't take it away from me. Carry this child and I'll do anything for you. Anything in the world."

Her face turns away from me, and she stares across the street in quiet contemplation. I can't force her to carry the baby. I can only hope to appeal to her humanity here.

When she turns to look at me, I'm not reassured. "Let me think about it. But I promise… we'll talk again before I decide. I'll hear you out, Wright. I owe you that."

"Thank you," is all I can say.

Everything else has been said, and the decision is up to her.

CHAPTER 2

Rachel

ADJUSTING THE REARVIEW mirror, I take another look at myself. My face is back to a normal color, but my eyes are still a little red. I pull some Visine out, give a few drops to each eye, and blink. The stuff is amazing, and the irritated little veins brought on by my unexpected crying jag ten minutes ago are erased like magic.

I take another look in the mirror, deciding I'm presentable enough to pass Kynan's muster.

I'd called him this morning to ask if I could come to his place to talk. As expected, his response was classic Kynan. "Bring donuts."

I grab the box of donuts from the passenger seat of my Maserati. Since I make fucking awesome money, I have all the toys. But I put my life in danger all the time, so I don't mind the splurge. Besides, I grew up with two doctors as parents, so I'm just continuing the same lifestyle I once knew—minus those few bohemian years I had living out of a suitcase in my early twenties.

After locking my car up, which is probably stupid as Kynan lives in a luxury gated community, I trudge across his sidewalk, lined with flowering cacti, to the front portico of his large Spanish colonial-style home. I ring the doorbell, and it takes him only moments to answer the door.

"Good morning," I say, trying to put on my brightest, most carefree face.

"Morning," he grunts, grabbing the donuts from me.

I follow him into his kitchen. He plops down on a counter island stool and pulls a chocolate-covered donut out. Dropping my purse and keys to the counter, I move around it to the Keurig and make a cup of coffee. I know Kynan's house well as he's about my closest friend in the world, and I've spent a lot of time here over the years.

As I grab half and half from his fridge, he asks, "Why have you been crying?"

Jolting, I whip my head around to look at him in disbelief. I know damn well my complexion and eyes give nothing away. "What makes you ask that?"

Kynan smirks and waves the donut. "You forget... I'm a former British commando. Reconnaissance is my middle name."

"Your middle name is Lee," I say dryly. I turn back to the fridge, hoping he doesn't see guilt on my face since I was, in fact, crying out in the car.

"I fucking watched you sit in the car for ten minutes

with your head bowed," he says with obvious delight, and my shoulders sag in defeat. "Then I saw you wipe your snotty nose and pop some Visine."

It's almost comical how his British accent make the words "snotty nose" sound almost refined, but I'm not in the mood to laugh.

With a sigh, I let the fridge door swing shut. I keep my back to him while I doctor up my coffee, using the rote actions to let me collect my thoughts. I came here intending to get advice, because I know that I can't be rational about my current predicament.

When I finally turn toward Kynan, he's halfway through his second donut. That he can eat unlimited carbs and sugars and maintain the chiseled body of a Greek god kind of makes me hate him. He just patiently stares at me, chewing on the sugary goodness.

"I'm pregnant," I say, dropping the bomb because there's no easing into something this monumental.

Kynan's eyes round with surprise. His jaw locks and he swallows, setting the rest of the donut on top of the box from which it came. Pushing the box aside, he rests his forearms on the counter, leaning slightly toward me to show I have his undivided attention.

"It happened in Paphos," I continue, dropping my gaze into my coffee. It's easier to look at right now. "With Wright."

"Wright?" Kynan blurts.

My eyes rise to meet his, and I lift my chin a little

defiantly. "Don't judge. It happened, okay?"

"Are you two... like together?" he asks hesitantly.

I shake my head before taking a quick sip of coffee. "No. It just happened. Emotions were high. Bourbon was involved. And we were fucking stupid for not using protection."

"Jesus." Kynan rubs his hand over the top of his head while he stares at the donut for a moment. When he looks back to me, he asks, "Does he know?"

"Yeah." I pace to the kitchen island, opposite of Kynan, and put my cup down. Mimicking him with my forearms to the granite, I lean toward him. "I told him last night."

"And what does he think?"

"I note you don't ask what I think," I say pointedly.

"Because I know what you think," Kynan replies blandly. "I've known you for almost thirteen years. Know you better than anyone probably. And you, love, don't want to have a baby. You don't want to involve your heart, nor impede your career, because your career is all you have in life."

Fuck... he nailed it.

"Wright wants me to keep it," I say morosely. "He wants to raise it."

"Not surprised," Kynan says dismissively. "He's a family man through and through."

"He's only twenty-six and has the rest of his life in front of him." My voice sounds so bitter, and I hate it.

"Why would he possibly want to ruin it?"

"Rachel," Kynan chastises, and I cringe over how guilty his tone makes me feel. "You know fucking well babies don't ruin anything."

I don't respond because there's no need to even voice it. Kynan knows the true source of my fear, and he's not going to let me pretend otherwise.

Thankfully, he doesn't pick at the scabs, but comes at me a different way. "You need to be careful, Rachel. It's not just your life that's being affected by this. I know the choices you face, and one path will end up devastating one of your teammates. Can you do that?"

I really don't think I can, but I was sort of hoping Kynan might give me permission to do so anyway. "So I have to give up a part of my life to carry this baby for him?"

"It's a few months. Big deal."

"Childbirth is painful," I say, completely offended that he'd try to diminish this.

"You've been through worse," he counters.

"Yes," I bite out angrily. "You do know I've been through worse."

Kynan winces slightly, and then has the grace to look semi-chagrined. He knows my worst is really, really bad. "I'm sorry. I know this is scary and the last thing in the world you wanted. But you're strong, healthy, and even if you don't want this child, Bodie does. You both made a mistake by not using protection, and he's apparently stepping up to the plate. Are you going to do the same?"

My entire being deflates when I realize I didn't even need to come over to Kynan's to talk this out. I knew what I was going to do, and he just helped me confirm it.

"You know I am," I say softly.

"That's my girl," he praises.

"What does this mean for me with The Jameson Group?" I ask hesitantly. When Kynan's eyes drop to look at my stomach, I realize I'd been subconsciously rubbing my belly.

Kynan's eyes drift back to mine. "I don't know exactly. We've never had a pregnant member on staff before. I'll have Doc McCullough refer you to a good OB/GYN, and you'll need to see what that doctor says."

I nod, my mood completely glum over the fact that at some point, I'm going to be out of commission. There's one thing Kynan is right about. My career is everything to me. It's what sustains and fulfills me. I have no clue what I'm going to do if I can't go on operations.

"Don't even ask me to do secretarial work," I mutter as I pick my cup back up. I take a sip as Kynan laughs at me.

"The minute you go on inactive status, I'll have you work on strategic planning with me. I know it's not getting your hands dirty, but you'll still be actively involved. Your brain and cunning are probably your best tools to be honest."

"Damn right I will," I snap, but I'm secretly relieved to hear him say that. Kynan doesn't dole out a ton of praise or affirmation, so it's nice to hear it right now.

Kynan chuckles and shakes his head. "Wow... our first Jameson baby. If it's a boy, you should name him Jameson. Or Kynan. That would be nice."

"That's up to Wright," I say with a pointed look over the rim of my cup. It's not going to be something I even need to wrap my head around.

I get a return grin, and it chafes he's amused at me.

"So," he says slyly, with a little wink. "You and Wright, huh? Can't say I saw that one coming."

"I didn't see it coming either." The petulance in my voice makes his chuckle go to a belly laugh. I roll my eyes. "Just stop. I was upset over Joram, had way too much liquor, and well... he was all hot looking and I needed the distraction."

"Was it good?" he asks. In normal circumstances, I should be offended. Yes, this man is my friend, but he's also my boss. And he's asking about a personal intimacy.

But I'm not, because Kynan and I used to be lovers before we settled into a good friendship *without* benefits. That was long ago, but there was a time I laid in bed with him and spilled secrets. He was by my side during some of my darkest days. While we haven't been carnal with each other in almost a decade—since I started work at Jameson as a matter of fact—he still has firsthand knowledge of my sex life. We can't exactly frequent the same sex club without seeing a few things.

"It was good," I admit, but that's not the full truth. It was spectacular, and that's surprising to me. I was totally buzzed from the alcohol and full of seething anger at myself. It should have been hard as hell for anyone to get me off, but damn if Wright didn't do it in just a few short minutes.

He'd thrown me on the bed and because I'd already been naked, his first move had been to shove his face between my legs. The first touch of his tongue on me and my back arched so high I thought I'd broken it.

Just minutes.

Minutes and a very talented mouth, and I was screaming out the first of three orgasms.

"Your face tells me all I need to know," Kynan says knowingly.

My face flushes red, and I wonder how long I'd zoned out thinking about that night with Bodie.

Wright.

I need to think of him as Wright.

Just a coworker and a teammate.

"Whatever," I growl under my breath, but then give Kynan a very bland look. "Like I said, it just happened. It was a onetime thing."

"If you say so," he intones in such a way that I know he doesn't believe me.

"I do say so," I say firmly.

"I believe you," he says soberly, but then his lips

break into a grin. "No, I don't. I just saw that look on your face. Whatever Wright gave you that night in addition to a baby blew your fucking mind. You're going back for more."

"Am not," I insist.

"Are too," he says like a five-year-old.

"He's too young for me," I argue.

"You dig that hole deeper, Hart. Keep telling me all the reasons you're not going to fuck Bodie Wright again, and I'm going to laugh in your face when it happens."

It won't, I think stubbornly. *No way.*

"Just drop it, McGrath," I tell him. "I've got more important things to worry about."

His expression sobers, and he nods. "Yeah, I know. And I've got your back. But just remember… nothing wrong with you and Wright hitting it together."

I really wish he hadn't said that.

CHAPTER 3

Bodie

MY CELL PHONE rings, and I roll slightly on the couch to nab it from the coffee table. My mom's pretty round face is on the screen, and I'm smiling when I answer. "And how is the best mom in the entire world doing today?"

Estelle Wright giggles into the phone. Most fifty-year-old women can't pull giggling off well, but my mom is lit from within by a natural sunny disposition. Practically anything that comes out of her mouth is joyful.

"Oh, you stop it," she chides, the distinctive sound of her beating something within a bowl coming over the line. The woman can never sit still.

"Whatcha making?" I ask, my stomach rumbling with the thought of my mom's home cooking.

"A birthday cake for Rebecca," she says, and I can imagine her now... her phone pressed between her shoulder and ear while she rests her big blue ceramic bowl against her stomach, perhaps whipping batter with a wire beater. She never uses an electric mixer, always preferring her own elbow grease instead.

"Her birthday's not until next weekend," I point out.

"Oh, I know," she huffs into the phone. "But she's a little princess and wanted a birthday cake today, so I capitulated."

I laugh deeply because that's so like my little niece. She's my sister Jennifer's daughter and is five going on thirty-five. Jennifer had her when she was just nineteen. It was an unplanned pregnancy with her high school sweetheart, but they've made it work. They live in the big farmhouse with my mom and dad, along with my twin brothers Jeff and Kurt, who are seniors in high school. Jennifer's husband works the farm with my dad.

"So, how are you?" my mom asks in an airy voice. We talk a few times a week when I'm not away on an operation. They're not overly long conversations, but they are quality.

"I'm good," I say as I sit up, throwing my feet up on the coffee table. "Was watching some old movie on TV. Just relaxing today."

"When are you going out on your next job?" she asks. The tiny tinge of worry in her voice is something she can never hide.

She doesn't know the exact details of my work, but she knows that some of it is quite dangerous. I could never lie to her about that, but it's something she's become slightly used to since I used to be a SEAL.

"I've got a concert security detail in a few weeks. Some pop princess I've never even heard of."

"Well, if you'd quit listening to that head-banging metal music, you might know," she says pertly.

"Yeah, Mom. I hear you. Broaden my horizons and all that. How's Dad doing?"

"He's fine," she says with a huff. "Went back to work too early if you ask me. Just got the soybean crop planted, and, of course, he did most of it himself with Chad's help."

Chad is Jennifer's husband. My dad had a hernia repair a few weeks ago, but I'm not surprised he's out on the tractor. When the planting has to happen, it has to happen because it's usually boxed in by spring storms. The window to get the seed into the ground is narrow.

"I'm sure he's fine." It's true. My dad is one tough son of a bitch, and one of the hardest-working men I know. A real salt-of-the-earth type of guy.

"Listen, honey," my mom says into the phone. "Jennifer's standing here. She wants to talk to you."

"Okay," I say, but my mom is already handing the phone off. Jennifer's voice comes through clearly.

"Hey, Bobo," she says sweetly.

I get a pang of longing for home from her use of my childhood nickname. I can't quite remember if Bobo is short for Bodie or brother from when she'd been just starting to talk as a baby, but she still calls me that to this day.

"What's up, Jenny Sue?" I tease, knowing she hates me to call her that. She's always preferred the more dignified Jennifer.

"I've got news," she says in a half-squeal, half-breathy sigh, totally ignoring my use of that horrid name.

"What?" I ask, amused by the mental image of her practically hopping in place to tell me something.

"I'm pregnant," she shrieks into the phone and I wince, pulling my cell away for a moment before putting it back to my ear. Her and my mom are laughing excitedly in the background. "Chad and I are pregnant. Three months. Baby will be here right before Thanksgiving."

"That's awesome, sis." My heart expands at the thought of adding a new niece or nephew to my crew of potential kids I can spoil. "So was this planned?"

"It was," she gushes with pride. "We didn't want to wait too much longer. We wanted Rebecca and the next kid to be fairly close in age."

For a moment, my knees go weak when I realize I could be having a kid within just a few months of Jennifer. My son or daughter would have cousins the same age, and they'd be as close as siblings I'd bet.

But I give my head a hard shake. I refuse to think about that because there's no sense wondering about "what if" until I know what Rachel wants to do.

"Will you be coming home for Thanksgiving or

Christmas?" Jennifer asks.

"Absolutely," I tell her with confidence. "I've got nothing scheduled right now, but I'll make sure to keep one of those holidays open so I can put on my uncle boots."

"Awesome, Bobo," she sighs into the phone, and I miss my sister greatly in this moment.

Fuck... I miss my entire family, but that's always been the way it is. When I decided to leave home for the military, having to be separated from those I loved most was my big sacrifice.

"Miss you, kiddo," I tell her gruffly.

"Miss you back," she says, and then adds, "Hold on. Mom wants to talk to you again."

There's a slight pause, and my mom is back on the line. "Hey, honey. So you'll come for Thanksgiving or Christmas?"

"Promise," I assure her, since I have the ability to decline any operation or detail presented to me. I didn't make it home last year for either holiday, so I'm going this year.

"Well, we miss you," she says.

Another pang of longing for home hits me. It's something I know will never go away. "Miss you, too, Mom," I mutter into the phone, my voice a little hoarse with emotion. "Tell Dad I said hello."

"Will do," she says softly, and I can even imagine a slight mist in her eyes. "Bye."

"Bye," I say and then disconnect the call.

Tapping my phone against my chin, I contemplate the holidays. Maybe I should go for both Thanksgiving and Christmas. I just need to let Kynan know soon so he can make sure to have my absence covered. In fact, I could take several weeks off and just stay there the entire time. I make good bank with The Jameson Group, and I can easily afford not to work for a month or two.

A soft knocking on my door startles me, and I turn to look at it. It's solid wood with three small panes of glass set at a diagonal, but I can't see who it is.

I walk around my couch to the door. When I get nearer to the glass, I can see Rachel standing on my front porch.

An electric zap of adrenaline hits me, because I know she's here to tell me something important. It's something that's going to change my life, one way or the other.

When she told me she was pregnant last night, there wasn't an ounce of hesitation when I said I wanted that kid. Even after a night of sleep and ruminating about it incessantly, that feeling hasn't changed. It would be hell to make it work, but I'd fucking do it.

I take a deep breath, let it out in a rush, and then open the door. She'd been looking out toward the road and spins around to face me. "Hey," she says as if she's surprised to see me standing in my own house. I chalk that up to nervousness.

"Hey," I say and then step back, sweeping with my

arm to silently invite her in.

She crosses the threshold, her eyes roaming the small interior of my house. "You really live out in the boonies, don't you?" she asks as she turns to face me.

"Not a city boy," I tell her. "Like the quiet and solitude."

Which is why I bought this little Pueblo-style ranch house that sits without another neighbor in sight. Nothing but scrubby desert as far as the eye can see with the Spring Mountains in the distance.

"Because you were raised on a farm?" she asks.

"Yeah, probably," I say with a shrug, never having given it much thought. I just know I prefer open spaces and natural scenery to concrete, glass, and steel. I like the sound of bugs at night versus honking cars.

Rachel doesn't have a purse, and nervously jangles her car keys in her hand. She looks around my living room again, craning her neck a bit to see past the half wall that separates it from my kitchen. My house is barely twelve-hundred square feet with only two bedrooms, but it's enough for me. I'm saving my money for something bigger and better one day. I always thought that meant when I was ready to settle down and start a family, but my life got a little messy in the last twenty-four hours, so who knows what the fuck it means now.

"Do you want something to drink?" I ask, and her head snaps back to me.

She gives a hard shake of her head. "No, I'm good."

"Want to sit down?" I motion her to the couch.

Rachel tucks a lock of hair behind her ear. She's worn it loose and shaggy today, doesn't have a speck of makeup on. Personally, it's when she's prettiest in my opinion.

With a tight smile, she walks over to the couch, sitting stiffly on the edge of the cushion. Her back is straight, head held confidently high. I think it's an act because she still nervously jangles her keys.

I take a seat on the other end of the couch, angling my body to her and planting my elbows on my thighs, which causes me to lean slightly into her space. I don't say a word, only look at her with what I imagine is unmitigated hope. At least, that's what the emotions swirling through my body indicate.

Please don't crush me, Rachel.

Rachel gives me another smile, this one a little pained. Her eyes go down to the keys. As if she's just realizing she's making noise with them, she grips them tighter in her palm.

"Um... I went and talked to Kynan a little bit ago, and got his advice," she says before slowly raising her face to mine. Her eyes are determined with an underlying layer of fear deep inside. "And... I'll carry the baby. Please don't think badly of me, but I don't want to raise it. I'm not ready for that."

There's no stopping the huge gush of pent-up air

inside of me, my lungs burning from the force of it.

"Thank you, Rachel," I say with so much gratitude. I'm not sure I've ever been this thankful for anything in my life. I'm swamped with utter fear now, yet I'm grateful to have it. "And no... I'd never think badly of you for that type of personal decision."

She nods, her expression guarded. "I'm not sure how to make this all work. I mean... there will be legalities later, and well, the pregnancy and how it will affect my work."

"I'd like to be involved in the pregnancy," I blurt. It's not something I allowed myself to think about last night and today, but now that there's actually going to be a baby continuing to grow in her, one who is made up of me, I want to experience every little fucking thing.

To my surprise, Rachel's body tightens, her voice coming out a little frosty. "And what do you mean by that?"

I blink, suddenly confused as to what that means. I give a helpless shrug. "I don't know. Um... doctor's visits, maybe? And if you were to need anything, I hope you'd ask me."

To my surprise, Rachel gives a tiny bark of laughter followed by a nervous snicker. She holds a hand up. "I'm sorry. I just don't know what in the hell I'm doing. I guess I had images of you wanting to rub my belly constantly or sing songs to it or something."

Her remark causes a genuine laugh to erupt from me.

We're both nervous and totally out of our depths.

"I promise not to do that," I tell her, but then quickly amend. "Unless you want me to."

She's the one to shrug this time. "I have no clue what I want. Maybe late-night ice cream runs?"

We share a look, and it's one I recognize. We've shared it before. It's the look of one teammate to another that says, "I got your back."

Impulsively, I reach out and snag her empty hand, giving it a very short squeeze. "We'll get through this."

Rachel lets out a shaky breath with another tiny laugh. "I know. I know we will."

"Rachel," I say, my voice going an octave deeper because of how much I mean it. "Really... thank you. I don't know what I would have done if you'd decided otherwise."

"Knowing you, Wright," she says with a pointed look as she pulls her hand away from mine. "You would have kidnapped me and kept me hostage until I'd given birth."

She's wrong about that because I'd never force her to do something she didn't want to. I would have just dealt with the loss, because what else could I have done?

Pushing up from the couch rather abruptly, Rachel looks down at me. "Look... I have to get going, but Doc McCullough is going to get me set up with an OB/GYN this week. I'll let you know when the appointment is."

I stand up and follow her to the door. "Yeah, sure...

okay. That would be great."

Rachel doesn't respond, just opens my front door. She starts to step through, but then hesitates as if struck by something. She turns to look back at me.

"How are you going to do this on your own?" she asks me hesitantly.

"I have no fucking clue," I tell her truthfully. "My gut instinct is to head back home to Nebraska with baby in tow. I can't continue this line of work and raise a kid."

Rachel just stares, as if my answer doesn't make sense to her.

So I ask her a question of my own, "You never want kids?"

Her eyes turn a little wistful. "I always thought I would if the timing was right. But I'm at a stage in my career right now where the timing is very wrong for me."

I nod in understanding. Rachel is very good at what she does. Part of the reason for that is because she "loves" what she does. I mean really loves her work. It's all she has in life, and it's her priority.

This disappoints me more than I care to admit, because if Rachel would just potentially be open to the idea of co-parenting with me, we could both continue to work at The Jameson Group. We'd never go on missions or details with each other again, but we could share in the responsibility of raising a child together and keep our careers.

Maybe she'll change her mind down the road.

Maybe she won't.

The only thing I know for sure is that I'm going to be a father in approximately seven and a half months.

CHAPTER 4

Rachel

MY SKIN IS itching. Prickles course up and down my spine. I'm unsettled. Ready to explode.

I'm looking for something. Anything, really. The only place I know to find it is in The Wicked Horse.

I prowl through The Social Room, my gaze sweeping around for potentials. Nothing catches my eye. My interest isn't piqued.

I make my way to my favorite room, The Silo. It's usually the first place I try since the most adventurous patrons tend to hang out there. When I enter, my eyes are immediately drawn to the perimeter rooms built of glass walls. They are filled with people fucking, and I wait for the familiar warmth of anticipation to overtake me.

Nothing.

The prickles on my skin turn to painful needles.

With a sigh, I turn toward the circular bar in the middle of the room and my eyes immediately land on

Kynan, who sits by himself. I happen to know The Silo is his favorite room, too, because he spends a lot of time here.

I make my way to him, and take the empty stool to his right. His head swivels, and he seems surprised to see me.

"Well, hello there, stranger," he drawls.

Turning my eyes briefly away from him, I tell the bartender, "A bottle of water, please."

Twisting back to Kynan, I ask, "Stranger? I just saw you at work today. And at your house just the day before that. I hardly think I'm being a stranger."

Kynan chuckles. "That's true. But you haven't been at The Wicked Horse for weeks. In fact, not since before you went on the Syrian mission with Bodie."

Has it really been that long?

"If I really wanted to get specific about it," Kynan continues in a taunting voice. "Not since the time you and Bodie hooked up while in Paphos."

My eyes narrow. "What are you trying to say?"

"You know what I'm saying. It's been over six weeks."

The bartender returns with my bottle of water, and I take it from him. "So what if it's been a long time?"

Kynan gives a casual shrug. "I just think it's interesting that you haven't fucked anyone since Bodie."

My head snaps his way. "Just because I haven't been in here doesn't mean I'm not fucking someone." That gets a resounding snort of disbelief from Kynan, which pisses me off. "For all you know, I have a boy toy stashed at my house. I could be fucking his brains out morning, noon, and night."

"Oh yeah," Kynan drawls. "If that's true, why are you here right now?"

I refuse to answer because it will only lead to his amusement. He likes to pretend he knows everything going on in the lives of his employees, and for the most part, he does. He's one of the most intuitive people I know, damn him. But I'm feeling too unsettled and on the verge of exploding with some type of unnamed anger, so it's best I don't engage with him. Besides, Bodie has nothing to do with my absence from The Wicked Horse.

Not really. I mean, he has been occupying my thoughts since that night we were together, but I can't give much credence to that. It was a phenomenal night of fucking that has left me bitter because I'm now knocked up. It certainly means nothing at all that my experiences here at The Wicked Horse have seemed beyond pale in comparison to that one night with him.

I chalk the sentiments up to some type of crazy pregnancy hormones going on within me.

Still, I hate myself intensely when I feel the need to ask Kynan, "Has Bodie been coming in?"

To Kynan's credit, he doesn't laugh. There's not even a teasing flash that I can detect in his expression. He just looks at me blandly, and asks me a question in return. "Why does it matter?"

Ugh, it doesn't matter. It absolutely does not matter.

Grabbing my water bottle, I rise from the stool. I won't give Kynan the satisfaction of knowing he's gotten to me, so I merely give him a cool smile. "I'm off to go prowl around. Happy fucking tonight."

Kynan jerks his chin upward in acknowledgment. But before I can turn fully away from him, he asks, "Have you scheduled an appointment with an OB/GYN yet?"

I nod. "Tomorrow, actually."

"Good. I'm sure you've got a lot of questions for the doctor."

A lump forms in the center of my throat, and I attempt to swallow past it with utter failure. All I can do is nod in response before turning to walk away.

Kynan's hand shoots out and encircles my wrist, bringing me to a halt. I crane my neck to look over my shoulder at him, raising one eyebrow in question.

"Rachel," he says softly. "It's going to be fine."

I appreciate his optimism. He knows the source of my fear, so he feels compelled to say that. But his words hold no weight with me because no one knows for sure that it will be. I don't want to talk about it any further, so I give him a warm smile along with the words he needs to hear so he can feel better. "Of course it will. I've got this."

Kynan studies me for a moment before releasing my wrist. He inclines his head and says, "Happy hunting."

I make my way back through The Silo and decide to try The Orgy Room. It's easy to get laid in there because all I have to do is insinuate myself into a group of naked writhing bodies. No one ever says no.

I enter the room, trying to open myself up to the myriad of sights and sounds that have never failed to get me in the mood. The Orgy Room is just one spacious room where people in various states of undress fuck in groups of two or more. Low-lying benches and chaises fill the floor, while focused beams of light project from the ceiling down onto them. Grunts and moans and screams of pleasure fill the air.

It does nothing for me.

Goddamn it.

I square my shoulders with resolve. The move pushes my tits up against the low scoop of the blood-red dress that barely covers my intimate bits. With my nearly black hair, it's the color that looks best on me. My eyes latch onto a group of three men and two women kissing and groping not ten feet from me. They are partially dressed, which suggests they are just getting started. One of the men looks up, and our eyes lock. He's very handsome with longish brown hair and a trimmed beard. He grins wickedly and crooks his finger.

I put some extra sway in my hips as I start to walk his way.

For the second time tonight, my wrist is captured by a large hand. Before I even turn to see who has me, the prickles that had been racking my skin with extreme agitation immediately dull.

When I look over my shoulder, I'm not surprised to see Bodie.

And God… why does he have to look so good? Well-fit jeans, charcoal gray V-neck that hugs his muscled torso. That freakin' mink-brown hair that seems messy and perfectly styled at the same time. It felt really damn good with my fingers running through it.

He's too young, Rachel, I tell myself so I quit thinking about him that way, but it sounds totally hollow. I've never been one to box myself in by a stereotype. If I did, I wouldn't be a member of an elite mercenary group since I'm a woman.

"What are you doing?" he asks, his hand locked tight on me.

A zing of lust pulses between my legs at the possessive tone of his voice. I have no clue why he feels he has the right to be possessive of me, but my body sure seems to like it.

A gamine smile spreads across my face, and I step into him. "Oh, come on, Bodie. You know what I'm doing. I'm getting ready to get fucked. It's why we come to The Wicked Horse, right?"

His chocolate-brown eyes look past me to the group I'd been headed toward before coming back to me. "If you want to get fucked, I'll be glad to do the honors. It's not like I can get you any more pregnant."

I gasp, but I don't know if it's from outrage or desire. I pretend I'm offended, though, and pull against his hold. "I don't need your help to get fucked."

Bodie's hand tightens. He gives me a little jerk, and I fall into his body. My free hand goes to his chest to steady myself. His heartbeat thunders under my palm.

"There are plenty of women in here for you, Bodie," I grit out. There's no doubt he's been fucking other women in here the last several weeks since our encounter, but I can't hold it against him. We had no claims on each other.

My head tilts way back to look at him, and the intensity of his gaze makes my legs go weak. I almost sag against him when he brings his free hand to my stomach. Fingers splayed, he presses it against me and murmurs, "That's my kid in there, so things have changed a bit. No one's dick but mine gets near him. Or her. Whichever."

"That's ridiculous," I sputter, now offended he would think he could dictate what my body can and can't have in it. I ignore the way my sex starts to throb.

Bodie puts his mouth near my ear. His lips tickle my sensitive skin, and his words cause my panties to get wet. "Come on, Hart. What we did was great, and you know it. I'll make it even better. I've been reading up on pregnancy, and I know your hormones are going crazy. I'll gladly fuck you anytime you want."

My clit starts to pulse, and I have to force myself not to spread my legs for him. I manage to huff out in feigned offense, "Not interested."

The hand on my stomach drops and dips under my dress. Before I can even think to slam my legs closed against him, he inches a finger under my panties and slides it through my wet folds. My knees buckle, and he holds me upright just by his hold on my wrist.

"All evidence to the contrary," he murmurs triumphantly.

I open my mouth to argue, but his finger slides into me deep. Nothing comes out but a long, needy moan. My head falls back, and my eyes flutter closed.

Bodie's mouth goes to my neck where his lips whisper against my skin. "Mmm. So wet for me, Hart."

"Not for you," I mutter even as my hips rotate to get him to move inside of me.

He chuckles, and the confidence in his voice is grating. "All for me."

Pulling his finger out, he presses the pad all slick with my juices against my clit and starts to torture me with tiny circles. I buck against him. He finally releases my wrist, only to bring that hand to my waist to pin me in place against him.

"Let's see how fast I can get you off," he drawls in a low voice. I raise my head, open my eyes, and glare at him defiantly. He grins back at me. "You can act like you don't like this all you want, baby, but I know different."

"Shut up, Wright," I growl, one hand going behind his neck. "And do what you promised."

His grin goes wider. "That's my girl."

I am *so* not his girl, but I almost cry in relief as his mouth crashes down on mine and his finger flutters against my clit, dipping periodically inside to get more slicked up.

I raise a leg, hook it around his just below his ass, and rock into him. He groans into our kiss, and then shoves two fingers into me deeply. Twisting his hand a bit, his thumb hits my clit. Within moments, I'm coming hard and crying into his mouth.

Bodie groans and picks me up, his fingers still lodged deep inside of me, the other hand supporting my ass. My legs lock around his waist and he walks me over to a wall, pinning me hard against it.

My hands dive to his jeans and I rip them open, pulling his swollen cock out. My thumb grazes the precum on the top briefly, but only because Bodie raises me up and settles my pussy against him. He plunges in at the same time he jerks me down, hammering home, and the air is knocked out of my lungs.

Tilting his head, he darts his tongue out, licking the tip of my ear before clamping his teeth on it. I growl and buck, but he starts to fuck me so hard I can only hang on for the ride. He grunts like an animal during every deep thrust, and another orgasm starts to curl inside of me.

"Mmm, Hart," he breathes hotly into my ear while his cock tunnels into me so deep I'm seeing stars. "Love this pussy."

God, I love his cock. And his words. And everything.

"You know what really gets me?" he pants as he continues to fuck me against the wall.

"What?" I manage to gasp, hovering on the edge of a brutal release.

"Your cunt is so sweet and tight, but I know that ass is going to be even tighter. Can't wait to feel that on my cock."

"Fuck," I groan as I start to come, completely embarrassed his words are what tip me over the edge. When a man's words have power over me, I know it means I'm in deep trouble, because, frankly… no man has *ever* provoked such a response with just his voice.

In this moment, as my orgasm consumes me, I realize I'm in over my head with this man. The pregnancy just complicates it more.

"Best of all…" he gloats as my body shudders in ecstasy. Plunging in hard, he strikes deep and goes still, groaning against my neck, "Is coming inside this pussy."

Bodie grinds against me, and I can feel his orgasm ripple up his back while he's coming. He curses and grunts, thrusting shallowly against me while my muscles contract to milk him dry.

My head drops to his shoulder, my hands going limp where I'd been holding on tight.

Fuck, that was good. So good.

God help me, I already want it again.

CHAPTER 5

Bodie

THE DOOR TO the waiting room opens, and Rachel walks in. She's wearing a pair of khaki cargo pants, a white tank top, and tennis shoes. Her black hair is pulled back in a stubby ponytail. When her eyes immediately lock on mine, I put the magazine entitled *Pregnancy Today* on the table beside me. She gives me a small smile before heading to the check-in desk.

After giving information to the receptionist, she makes her way over to me and sits down with a heavy sigh in the chair to my right. The waiting room is filled with women, many of whom have a partner with them.

She leans toward me and whispers, "How long have you been here?"

"About fifteen minutes," I tell her. "I'm always habitually early to appointments, though."

She nods, lacing her hands in her lap.

"Are you nervous?" I ask.

She shakes her head. "Not really. Depending on what

we learn here today, though, I reserve the right to change my answer."

A low laugh leaves me, and I reach over to take one of her hands in mine. She jerks in surprise, and then looks at me with wide eyes as I bring her hand to my mouth. I press my lips to the tips of her fingers. "Thank you again for letting me be a part of this, Rachel. It means the world."

I'm utterly charmed when her face flames crimson. She snatches her hand back and clenches them in her lap once again.

I'm not sensing any awkwardness from Rachel about last night. I tried my damnedest to get her to come home with me from The Wicked Horse, but she was having none of it. I then tried to get her to take me home with her, but she was equally as stubborn. She's clearly struggling to establish some type of boundary between us, but damn if I'm going to let that happen.

We've fucked twice now, both times beyond amazing. She's carrying my child. I'm going to be a part of this pregnancy, so we are going to be spending time together. I intend to push her boundaries as hard as I can because when it boils right down to it, I'm still holding out hope that she might want to be a part of our baby's life.

Not to mention… the benefits of fucking Rachel over the next several months are unparalleled. It's true that I'd had sex with other women at The Wicked Horse since Rachel and I were together, but why wouldn't I? She and I had no commitment to each other, and we'd thought it would be a onetime-only thing. But knowing she's pregnant with my kid, God help me... I fucking want her bad. If I have to go a little alpha to keep her underneath me, I'm going to do it.

The door off the waiting room opens, and a nurse steps out. She looks out and says, "Rachel Hart."

Rachel jolts, and her head snaps up to look at the nurse. I push from my chair, pulling Rachel up by her elbow. "Here we go," I say with a squeeze.

We're led to a room that has an examination table with stirrups sticking out the end. There's a short counter with the sink and cabinets above it and a tiny chair in the corner, as well as a rolling stool for the doctor to sit on. I note a medical illustration on the wall that shows the stages of pregnancy, each drawing of the woman and the baby inside advancing in size during each trimester.

"Dr. Anchors is running just a little bit behind schedule," the nurse says while she pulls a paper gown from one of the cabinets. "Go ahead and remove all of your clothing, then put this on. He shouldn't be much more than fifteen or twenty minutes."

"Thank you," Rachel mutters as she takes the gown.

When the nurse closes the door, Rachel moves over to the chair in the corner and sets her purse down. She proceeds to mechanically remove her clothes, seemingly not bothered I'm in the room and watching. Since I've already seen her bare body up close and personal, she must not mind, and I'm certainly enjoying the view.

Rachel is a spectacularly built woman. She's tall and lithe, with toned muscles. Her stomach is flat, and I wonder when that will change. Her breasts are large and full, and I know they'll swell further. Once Rachel told me she was going to carry the baby, I'd scoured the internet and became quite versed in pregnancy. Since I intend to have my mouth on those breasts, I can gauge her discomfort by how she responds to me biting her nipples.

The thought causes my dick to thump in my pants. I have a feeling that is going to be a major problem for me in the months to come when I'm around her.

When Rachel has the gown wrapped around her body, she sits on the end of the exam table and crosses her feet at her ankles.

"Did you sleep good last night?" I ask, coming to stand beside her.

Shrugging, she picks at the paper covering her legs. She's being awfully withdrawn, and that just won't do. Particularly if she's having doubts about what we did at the club.

I scoot in closer and bend my head down to murmur, "Well, I couldn't get to sleep last night. Not thinking about the way you came all over my cock."

Her head snaps up, and she turns to glare at me. My

return smile is lazy and filled with mischief.

"Had to jack off because thinking about you made my dick so hard," I tell her with a grin.

I thought perhaps my teasing would make her angry, but I'm more than thrilled to see her eyes dilate slightly. She swallows hard. I step up to the edge of the table, and place my right hand just behind her ass so I can lean into her. Tilting my head, I nuzzle her neck. "And just so you don't forget, Rachel, I'm the only one fucking you."

My lips move, and then press against the skin just above her collarbone. I smile when she hisses, "That's fine. We'll fuck each other's brains out until this baby comes. But I don't want anyone to know."

I lift my head and stare down at her with an amused smile. "Why are you so bent out of shape about the idea of us together?"

She brings a palm to my chest and pushes against me. "I'm not bent out of shape. I just don't like someone up in my space all the time."

Laughter rumbles from deep within my chest, and I give her a chiding shake of my head. My hand goes to her bare knee, and starts sliding up her leg underneath the gown. The crisp paper crackles and rasps against her skin as it moves up. I can feel goose bumps as my hand reaches mid-thigh.

Rachel's legs slam together, trapping my fingers between them.

"Stop it," she growls.

I flex my fingers, giving her leg a squeeze. "You like me all up in your space."

"No, I don't," she insists. She then actually sniffs prissily at me and adds, "If we're together, I say when it's going to happen."

"Oh, now, Hart," I murmur with a dark laugh, pushing my hand higher up her leg despite the fact she's clamping her thighs together. She's no match for my strength. "I'm just going to have to prove you wrong about that."

Rachel slams a hand around my wrist in a pitiful attempt to stop me. She snarls like an aggrieved kitten, "We are in a fucking doctor's office for God's sake, Bodie."

I step around the end of the table. Bringing my other hand into action, I pull her legs apart. I step in between them until my half-hard dick presses against the padding. Leaning in, I brush my lips across her mouth and whisper, "Doctor's running a little bit late. We have time to fool around."

"I am not fooling around with you in a doctor's office," she says haughtily, bringing her hands to press into my chest.

I might have taken her seriously if instead of trying to push me away from her, she didn't flex her fingers into my shirt as if she wants to hold me close.

Now that was a mistake, Rachel.

I lean into her hard, pushing her torso all the way

back into the incline of the table, which has her sitting at about a forty-five degree angle. My tongue slips inside her mouth, tasting coffee and cinnamon gum. Rachel gives a tiny huff of frustration, but then she's kissing me back.

My smile against her mouth is triumph. Because she is so responsive, I bet I could make her come about five different ways before the doctor gets in here. My hands go to her ass. I pull her to the edge of the table, to where her bare pussy is pressed up against my denim-covered erection. I bet she's wet. I bet she'll leave a wet spot.

Rachel moans. Her hands go to my hips, pulling me in closer.

I know damn well I'm not going to get away with fucking her before the doctor comes in, but I bet I could eat her pussy hard and fast with my hand over her mouth to muffle her screams of pleasure.

Yeah, that's what I'm going to do.

My plans are dashed when the door to the examination room opens, and a male doctor in his mid-forties steps in. He has dark hair, parted straight and evenly combed. His black-framed glasses make him look very smart and accomplished.

Rachel gives a yip of embarrassment and I immediately pull back, dragging the paper down to cover her legs. Rubbing the tips of my fingers over my mouth, which is still tingling from that kiss, I turn to face the doctor with a sheepish grin.

He blinks at us from behind his frames and actually apologizes, "Oh, God... Sorry to have interrupted you."

Chuckling, I step away from the examination table and move to Rachel's side. "Hey, we're on your time, Doc. We just got a little carried away with each other while we were waiting for you."

The doctor laughs. "I was running late but when I saw you were the patient Henry McCullough sent over, I jumped you up in the queue, so you didn't have to wait for me."

Guess that's one of the perks of working for The Jameson Group.

He shakes each of our hands. "I'm Bill Anchors. And you must be Rachel Hart and Bodie Wright?"

"That would be us," Rachel says with a nervous laugh.

Dr. Anchors turns to the sink and washes his hands. "Today, I'll examine you, and then we're going to talk about what the game plan will be to monitor you through your pregnancy."

Rachel looks at me, and I give her a reassuring smile.

Dr. Anchors turns from the sink and takes a seat on the rolling stool. After snagging a pair of latex gloves from a box on the counter, he puts them on with practiced efficiency.

He rolls the stool up to the edge of the exam table. "Go ahead and put your feet in the stirrups and scoot down to the edge of the table. I'm just going to give you a quick pelvic examination."

I take a few steps back to stand near Rachel's shoulders as she does what the doctor requests. She stares at the ceiling blankly while the doctor squirts some lube on his finger and proceeds to insert it inside of her. Rachel flinches from the invasion, and my hackles rise. Not because another man has his hand between her legs, but because it's causing her discomfort. But I know this is part of his job, so I'm going to make it mine to try to ease that for her.

Putting my hand on her shoulder, I give it a squeeze. "You are seriously like the most beautiful and sexy woman I have ever known."

Rachel's head snaps my way and her eyes lock onto mine, filled with disbelief.

I nod encouragingly. "Seriously, Hart. All the guys have their tongues hanging out at you behind your back. If you ever want to stop being a mercenary, you could totally be a supermodel."

Rachel rolls her eyes and growls, "Will you seriously just shut the fuck up, Bodie?"

Dr. Anchors pulls his hand away with a suppressed chuckle and rolls his chair toward the garbage while pulling the latex gloves off. My hand goes behind Rachel's back and I help her sit up, bending down to whisper in her ear, "I'm not going to lie, I was trying to distract you. But I'm not lying about you being the most beautiful and sexy woman I know."

Rachel's face flushes. In that moment, it's obvious not many men have whispered sweet nothings to her. I find that to be very sad and in need of remedy for sure.

"Okay," Dr. Anchors says as he stands from the stool. He leans against the counter and crosses his arms over his chest. "Everything looks and feels good on your examination. Going to run some bloodwork and get a urine test to get some baseline readings. Assuming those all look good, you won't need to come back to see me for another thirty days. You'll start coming to see me biweekly at the end of your second trimester."

"And that's it?" I ask incredulously.

Dr. Anchors gives me a reassuring smile. "That's pretty much it. Not much to do during the first trimester. We'll do your first ultrasound at sixteen weeks, and we should be able to check the baby's gender at that point. Although given the fact that you're thirty-five, Rachel, you'll need to be thinking if you want to get some advanced testing."

"Advanced testing?" she asks hesitantly.

"Amniocentesis for starters," Dr. Anchors says. "There are a variety of tests we can do to check for abnormalities of the brain and spinal cord or genetic conditions. You two can discuss it and decide if you want to go that route. I've got some pamphlets that describe what each of the tests are and what they look for."

"Okay," Rachel says. She sits up straighter on the table, wrapping her arms tight over her stomach as if she's protecting the baby. Shooting me a quick glance, she then looks back to the doctor. "If it's possible, Dr. Anchors, I would like to be able to talk to you privately."

A zap of what feels like electricity skitters up my spine in surprise over her request, particularly because there's no mistaking the slight hint of worry in her voice. She's not looking at me, though. Her gaze is pinned on the doctor.

He gives her a warm smile. "Of course. That's not a problem."

I want to object because I don't want cut out of any discussion, particularly if there is something worrying Rachel. She says she's going to go through with this pregnancy for me, but what if she's having second thoughts?

Her hand comes down on top of mine, and she gives me a squeeze. "Bodie… it's just personal stuff I want to talk to him about. I haven't changed my mind about anything."

Relief floods through me because I hear the truth in her words, and I trust her. I nod and bend down to brush my lips over her cheek. "Okay. I get it. I'm just going to wait for you in the waiting room."

"Thank you," she says softly. "I won't be too long."

I shake Dr. Anchors' hand before leaving Rachel in the room to ask whatever secret questions she has, hoping she will eventually confide in me what has her worried so I can help her get through it.

CHAPTER 6

Rachel

I MAKE MY way down an empty corridor of gray concrete flooring and white cinderblock walls. I'm not particularly fond of security details, even less so when they're of some diva pop princess whose highest risk is getting stampeded by thirteen-year-old girls. It's not exciting enough for me and it's below my comprehensive skill set, but at least they'll have me perched in the catwalk that runs above the stage with a rifle. This pop star has had what have been deemed to be credible death threats, and while metal detectors are used at the venue, they're not foolproof. Her manager felt that adding specialized security through the Jameson Group was a wise use of her money, and I probably agree. I'm on the team covering tonight's Los Angeles concert. Another team will meet her in Houston for her next one.

Still… I'd rather be running black ops in a foreign country or protecting an important government official. Those are the jobs that gets my juices flowing, and make me feel vital and important.

I'm on this detail because I volunteered for it, and I volunteered for it because I don't know how many job details I'll be getting over the next few months given my pregnancy. Dr. Anchors and I discussed that privately.

I didn't want Bodie involved because I don't want him to know I've been pregnant before and had it end in a miscarriage, an event I still blame myself for to this day, despite being told repetitively by medical personnel that it hadn't been my fault.

But I know a part of it was due to the lifestyle I'd led at the time. I know it down in my bones, so I have to tread very carefully with how I treat my body over the next few months. I should keep stress to a minimum as well.

I decide to check on the various hospitality rooms they have set up in the concert venue. There's one for the star of the show—an incredibly skinny girl of seventeen named Janie March, who wears outrageously miniscule outfits and sings into a headset microphone, which, in my opinion, only Madonna can make cool. There's also one for the media and another for music industry VIPs. There will be someone from Jameson in each room following the concert. Our team for this detail totals eight, including Bodie, who I've hardly seen since we arrived a few hours ago. I have my perch set up, and I won't ascend until the venue doors open.

I check Miss March's room first. She's in there with

her own security as well as Hannah Miles. Hannah is a retired Chicago cop who still needs to work to support her husband's gambling needs since they moved to Vegas. She's been with Jameson for four years now. She nods at me when I pop my head in, and I return it.

As I head toward the VIP room just down the hall, I'm surprised to hear Bodie and Cage's voices coming through the open doorway. They're probably just hanging out in there since they'll both be in the stage wings during the concert, those two being the ones who would swoop Miss Miles off stage if something were to happen. There's a well-constructed plan that was developed between our team and hers weeks ago to ensure her utmost safety.

When I turn the corner, I halt when I hear my name—definitely Bodie's voice. That first zing of adrenaline that I've caught him talking about us immediately gives way to relief as I realize he's talking business.

"Hart could pick any shooter off from anywhere in this colosseum from her perch," Bodie says, and is that… pride in his voice over my abilities?

"I'd sure as fuck hope so," Cage says with a snort. "Her Olympic medals are decent credentials in my opinion."

My hand comes to my mouth, so I don't snicker out loud while they talk about me. I press against the wall about three feet from the open door, and shamelessly listen.

I don't talk about my Olympic experience much, although everyone at Jameson knows I competed. It's not that I'm not proud of my accomplishments—because I totally am—but it was just so long ago. These days, there's better crops of young athletes coming through that would smoke me all over the place.

I was a winter athlete and competed in the Biathlon, which combines cross-country skiing with rifle shooting. I attended the Games when I was seventeen, and again when I was twenty-one. I competed in the 15-km individual and the 12.5 km mass start events, receiving three silvers and a gold between the two, and then I was just done. I was tired of the grueling training regimen, which seemed almost exotic as I grew up in the sport because it kept me away from home and traveling all over the world. But then it hadn't been fun anymore and, despite my coaches having a cow, I retired at twenty-one.

Of course, my skills with a rifle translated into this type of work. A biathlete can hit a target less than two inches in diameter from a hundred and sixty feet while exhausted, out of breath, and laying prone on the snow-covered ground. My current rifle is a little better, though. The CheyTac M200 Intervention can hit a target from twenty-five hundred yards, so yeah... better toys with The Jameson Group.

"She's smokin' hot, though," Cage says, and I lean toward the door to listen more closely. "I'd love a crack at her, but she doesn't give anyone in our group the time of day. But I bet Kynan's had her at least once. They've known each other forever and are as thick as thieves."

This type of talk should bother me, but it doesn't. I know it happens. I've developed a thick skin. I can never let anyone know I've taken offense because, frankly, I'm playing in a world that's heavily dominated by men. They don't want to work in a dangerous situation with someone who lets emotions rule them or where they can't just be their disgusting pig selves at times.

But I do feel apprehension take root deep within me, because I don't like this conversation happening with Bodie. He knows me carnally and he's gotten me pregnant, two facts I do not want spread about. The pregnancy is going to come to light eventually, but I'd rather not have to explain the thing with Bodie to anyone.

I'm completely tense while I wait to see how Bodie handles this. Cage Murdock is his best friend, and they are tight. I know they talk about this shit because all guys do.

"Have some respect," Bodie says in a low but neutral voice that barely carries through the door. "She's our teammate."

I'm warmed through to my core by his protectiveness of me.

"Come on," Cage says teasingly, and I can almost imagine him nudging Bodie in the ribs with a knowing wink. "Don't tell me you haven't looked at her and—"

"I said have some fucking respect," Bodie snarls, and I jump at the anger saturating his words.

"Jesus," Cage mutters apologetically. "I'm sorry. Don't get your panties in a twist."

I spin away from the doorway and walk quickly back the way I came. I don't want to hear anymore, and I've heard enough. When I told Bodie I wanted to keep this secret, I trusted his word he wouldn't tell anyone. What I just heard was affirmation that my trust was well placed. If he were going to tell anyone about us hooking up or about me being pregnant, it would be Cage.

Clearly, he hasn't.

It also confirms we weren't seen together that night at The Wicked Horse. I didn't think we'd been, but if we had, the rumor mill would have been churning hard. Cage also would have said something.

I smile as I realize Bodie truly has my back. He's always had it when we're working together, but it's nice to know he has it on the other side.

He had it when we were at Dr. Anchors' office day before yesterday. No woman likes to get a pelvic exam. I hated myself when I flinched, because I don't like showing weakness. But damn if Bodie didn't see it, and then immediately started telling me all kinds of horse shit about me being beautiful and sexy. I didn't give any credence to the actual words, but I did give him a hell of a lot of bonus points for trying to distract me.

God, did I need it, too. More than just during that pelvic exam, the entire visit I'd been strung tight. And my talk with Dr. Anchors went no differently than my talk with the doctor who'd treated me when I miscarried thirteen years ago.

After Bodie left, I just bluntly told the doctor, "I've been pregnant before, contrary to the history form I filled out. I miscarried at nine weeks, and I need to do things differently this time."

He'd nodded at me in understanding, not asking why I'd left that information off the intake. I'm sure he figured out I didn't want Bodie to know. Instead, he replied, "What do you mean 'do things differently'? What did you do the last time that you think might have attributed to you losing the baby?"

It was obvious what the good doctor was thinking. Perhaps drugs. Maybe alcohol.

Not exactly, but not all that far from the truth.

"I was not good to my body for many years," I told him. I explained briefly about the brutal training I went through from my early teens through my retirement from the Olympics at twenty-one. After that, I hadn't been any better to my body. I channeled my need for thrills by moving from Olympic competition to the rush of adrenaline-pumping activities like skydiving, base jumping, and extreme climbing.

For almost a full four years after I left the Olympics, I traveled the world and lived like a bohemian bum, moving from one thrill to the next. I slept in cheap hotels or on friend's couches. I only had with me what I could carry in a duffel bag, always seeking bigger thrills, more dangerous adventure. I ate poorly and slept even shittier. In fact, it's how I met Kynan... base jumping off Angel Falls in Venezuela. I was jumping with a parachute. He went before me and jumped with a wingsuit. I saw him zip away, knowing jumping with a parachute was going to be way too boring for me.

What started then was a friendship that spanned many years, and is still going strong to this day. We were friends first because I was involved with someone else. Later, when I was unattached, we screwed around. When we could, we'd meet up to experience death-defying jumps or swimming uncaged with Great Whites. We'd fuck like crazed animals, and then we'd go on our way. We'd keep in touch with periodic emails or calls. It was a good friendship with a great benefits package while it lasted, but it was never exclusive.

It stopped when Kynan brought me on board to The Jameson Group. Of course, he didn't own it back then. Jerico Jameson did, and I had to pass his muster first. But when I accepted the job, we both knew we couldn't be involved sexually since he was in a position of authority over me.

And that was fine by me. It was just casual anyway.

So I told most of this to Dr. Anchors. The adrenaline and stress of my lifestyle. The poor nutrition and running my body into the ground. Always traveling and never resting. How I hadn't even known I was pregnant until I miscarried because my period was never regular.

That I miscarried within hours after a harrowing bungee jump off the Macau Tower in China.

Dr. Anchors listened to me patiently, which included a rundown of my more dangerous work with The Jameson Group.

When I ran out of steam, he said, "Rachel… just because you miscarried once, it doesn't mean it will happen again. And there is no way of knowing why you miscarried. It could have been one thing, or it could have been several factors, but the truth is that miscarriages are all too common in the first trimester."

That didn't make me feel better. Nothing would make me feel better, because no one could ever know the devastation it had caused me. Well, no one but Kynan. He had been in Macau, too, and he went to the hospital with me when I started bleeding badly. The boyfriend who had accidentally gotten me pregnant weeks before with a broken condom was long gone. He had never been long-term material anyway, so there was no reason to even track him down and tell him.

Yes, Kynan watched it all and let me cry on his shoulder, a vulnerability no one had ever seen before, nor has anyone since. Then he offered me a new path to pull me away from my grief.

The Jameson Group.

And here I am, repeating things all over again.

I make it to the stage, intent to climb the catwalk above for another check. I won't be moving my rifle up there, which is currently locked in our cargo van outside, until just before the doors open.

I put my foot on the bottom rung of the ladder that connects to the scaffolding above when I hear Bodie behind me. "Hey... Hart. Wait up."

Christ, he looks yummy in black cargo pants, a tight black t-shirt with the Jameson logo on the front pocket in white, and a holster with a Glock on his hip.

"What's up?" I ask in a cool tone. Him calling me Hart rather than Rachel tells me this is business.

He walks right up to me, but rather than stopping a respectable distance from me, he backs me up into the ladder, his hands coming to hold the rungs by my head and caging me in. Bodie dips his head and murmurs, "Tonight after we wrap up here... I'm coming to your room."

A shiver of anticipation runs up my spine, but I act offended. "What makes you think—"

"You've ignored me for two days," his deep voice rumbles right over me. "Ever since the doctor's office. I don't like being ignored."

This is true. We had a nice but brief chat after I talked privately to Dr. Anchors, and I told Bodie when the next appointment would be. Then we left in separate cars. I haven't seen him until today, even though he'd texted me the last two nights telling me he was at The Wicked Horse waiting for me.

There was some hesitation on my part because I didn't want to risk being seen by anyone else in the group. Mainly, though, I just avoided him because I don't want to be a "thing" together. I want to keep it as causal as can be, and that means we don't see each other every night.

The longer I drag this conversation out, the better the chance someone will stumble upon us in this intimate pose. Truth is that I want Bodie again, and tonight would be perfect. We're staying in L.A. after the concert, and don't fly out until morning.

"Fine," I say before slipping out from between him and the ladder. "Come to my room, and we'll get it on."

Bodie snickers and steps back into me. I hold my ground, refusing to even lean slightly away. His lips come very close to mine, but don't touch. His breath whispers over me, and I have to press my legs together when he says, "You know, Hart… there was a part of me that was kind of hoping you'd fight me a little. I was looking forward to making you submit."

"In your dreams," I mutter.

Bodie laughs and steps away from me. He gives me a quick wink and turns on his heel, walking away from me with a confident strut.

Maybe I'll put up a little bit of a fight tonight. I never mind being overpowered in the bed.

CHAPTER 7

Bodie

NOT SURE I'VE ever seen anything more perfect than Rachel Hart opening her hotel door to me stark-ass naked.

Beautifully, artfully naked without an ounce of shame. She's fresh out of a shower, and her hair is a million times blacker all slicked back and wet. It exposes with more clarity the cut of her cheekbones and the fullness of her lips. Her eyes blaze with need and her hands reach for me, snagging the waistband of my jeans.

I pull my shirt off in a hurry. She helps me out of my shoes and pants.

There's no gradual seduction of my cock. It's concrete hard and ready for her, but I've got something else planned first.

Batting Rachel's hands away when she reaches for it, I pick her up and carry her to the bed. I toss her down and then take her by the ankles, sliding her to the edge of the mattress. One hand goes to the back of a thigh. I push it up high and outward, spreading her. My other hand goes right in between, dragging an index finger through the lips of her sex.

Rachel lets out a huff of a pleasure, and her hips tilt. I press the very tip inside of her, find her soaking wet, and then withdraw. I just wanted to know if she was as fucking turned on right now as I am, and we haven't even kissed. We've only anticipated being together.

Now it's time to make her feel good.

I sink to my knees on the floor, push her legs further apart, and slam my mouth on her pussy. Rachel doesn't wax, but she keeps herself very trimmed. My tongue easily finds her swollen clit, and she grunts from the first contact.

My lips circle the sensitive flesh, suck lightly. When I release, I murmur against her, "Mmm. You taste fucking good, Hart. Like sweet baby mama."

She snorts.

Another tiny lick and her hips shoot off the bed. "You're so sensitive. Is that a pregnancy thing?"

I look up at her to find her watching me with glazed eyes. When my words penetrate, she starts to laugh. I give her a wink and dive back down, stabbing my tongue inside her pussy.

"Bodie," she barks out, her hands coming down to fist my hair hard.

I fuck her hard and deep with my tongue a few times, then lave softly at her sensitized clit. She tries to push her pussy into my mouth, but I pull back. When she settles, I give her a little of what she wants. When she starts getting greedy, I slow it down.

Finally, when she's begging me and pushing hard on the back of my head for me to make her come, I batter at her with my tongue, teeth, and lips until she's screaming out her release. I don't stop, working her down gently until she's a writhing mass of tortured nerves under me.

Laying my chin on the top of her pubic mound, I look up her body. Her tits are big, her nipples pebbled hard. She lifts her head and looks down at me blearily.

"You're so fucking beautiful all spread out under me, completely boneless," I whisper. She rolls her eyes, and her head falls back to the mattress.

I lift my head, look down at her pussy. My dick is aching to slide in.

My hands glide down her inner thighs, and I peel her open with my thumbs to stare. It's fucking gorgeous.

"This cunt, Rachel," I say softly, and her head lifts back off the bed. I glance at her, and then back down to my prize. "All swollen and dripping wet. All mine."

I tap on her clit, which is protruding a bit, begging for more action. Rachel hisses in response.

Not able to stand it a moment more, I rise from the floor and my hands go under Rachel's ass. I lift her from the mattress to drive deep into her.

Slick, hot, tight as fuck.

"Mmm... mmm," I can't help but groan in absolute

relief.

"Oh, God," Rachel mutters.

She looks amazing from this angle. Fingers clutching onto the bedspread, ass in the air, and her eyes burning as they laser into mine.

I slowly pull out, almost to the tip, watching my cock shine with her juices. When it becomes too unbearable, I plunge back in.

"Yes," she whispers fiercely, and I'm done.

I let her drop to the bed, fall onto her, and push back into her deep. My mouth comes down on hers, and my torso flattens against her. My hands grope and clutch, finally finding hers, and I lace our fingers together as I pull them above her head.

And while I'm touching every single part of her I possibly can, I start to fuck her furiously hard. I race for the end and gladly plunge over when I can feel her start to contract around me, crying out her second orgasm.

I punch my cock in deep one last time, grab her lower lip with my teeth, and growl out the world's best fucking orgasm while I shoot what feels like gallons of cum into her.

"Jesus," I groan against her mouth before rolling to my side. She has no choice but to come with me since my arms encircle her. I lift her leg over my hip and keep myself planted inside of her while I let my heart rate come back down to a normal level.

Rachel is silent, but she seems content to lie like this.

Her arm is draped lazily across my ribs, her face pressing into my neck. I'm content to stay this way as well, because I've never been averse to cuddling.

Something about the fact that my stomach is pressed against the stomach of the woman who is carrying my kid makes it special. If I weren't so comfortable right now, I'd want to stick my hand in between us and touch her belly. That would probably freak her out, though, so I abstain.

"Is this weird?" she asks, and the sudden sound of her voice startles me.

Leaning back so I can look her in the eye, I ask, "Is what weird?"

"What we just did?"

"Sex?"

"Well, yeah," she says almost hesitantly, as if she's now doubting that what she thought might be weird actually isn't at all. "I mean... we're coworkers. We've known each other for a few years. Now we're fucking. It's just weird, right?"

"I'm pretty sure the weirdness comes from the fact we're pregnant," I say with a chuckle. "The fact we're fucking is just a bonus."

She gives a reluctant smile along with a chastising look. She wants me to be serious, but I'm feeling too replete and high on amazing sex to be.

I decide to change the subject. "Did you fill Kynan in on everything we learned at Dr. Anchors?"

Turns out, between our meeting with him and whatever Rachel discussed with him privately, there just wasn't a whole lot. We were loaded down with literature on what to expect throughout the pregnancy, and had a good idea of what would happen on the subsequent follow-up visits. Dr. Anchors said there weren't many limitations on Rachel this first trimester—at least physically for her job. She told me she'd described to him what all she did. Technically, she was as fit and physically sound to perform her job now as she was before she got pregnant. Of course, this might not hold true two months from now when she starts to show, and the baby could be more susceptible to injury as it grows.

"I filled him in," Rachel says. By the tone of her voice, I'm thinking it wasn't an enjoyable conversation.

"What's he have a problem with?" I ask.

She gives a tiny shrug. "I guess he's just worried about the general risk of sending a pregnant woman on the more dangerous ops."

"Is he going to sideline you?"

Rachel doesn't answer me directly. Instead, she asks. "Do you think I should be sidelined? I mean, this *is* your kid. What are your worries?"

I'm totally surprised by her graciousness toward my feelings on the matter, but I'm also careful in my answer. "Rachel... you know your body better than I ever could. I understand the risks, but pregnancy isn't a disability. I guess right now at this stage, I don't believe there's much you can't do. So, unless you're worried about something…"

I let myself trail off, leaving it up to her to complete that sentence.

Chewing on her lower lip, Rachel considers this for a moment. "There are risks in everything."

"You could be hit by a bus tomorrow crossing the street."

She tries to pull away from me, but I hold her tight in place. "I'm a higher risk because of my age."

"Because of the age of your egg, not because of what you do for a living," I point out. I'd read all the literature they sent home with us and some additional stuff online. "I don't think you need to stop living your life because you're pregnant. I think you need to look at each mission, where it will be, and what the actual risk is. You can make decisions as opportunities are put in front of you."

Her lips tilt up in an attempted smile, but the light of it doesn't reach her eyes. She's conflicted about something, and I'm wondering if this has to do with what she wanted to talk to Dr. Anchors about. She said it was about personal female stuff, and I took her at face value. But now…

"Do you know how Kynan and I met?" Rachel asks softly, and the change of subject and fondness in her voice throws me completely off.

"Um… no. I don't believe so."

Rachel wiggles slightly, not to pull completely away, but to put enough distance between us so she can look at me without craning her neck backward.

"After I retired from the Olympics, I spent a few years just traveling around the world and indulging in all my adrenaline-rush whims."

"Adrenaline-rush whims?" I ask with a laugh. "Now that's a term I've never heard before."

She chuckles. "Skydiving, bungee jumping, free diving, base jumping, rock climbing. You name it, I did it. The scarier the feat, the more I wanted to do it."

"Damn, Hart," I murmur, dropping my hand to her ass and giving a playful squeeze. "That's kind of hot."

She grins. "I met Kynan just about an hour before he dove off Angel Falls. Just over thirty-two hundred feet. We became fast friends after I jumped off after him."

I can't help the low whistle of respect and appreciation that blows through my teeth. I like the flow of adrenaline, but not sure I like it that much.

"I don't always appreciate danger," she says. This time, the smile is gone from her face. She's being as serious as she can possibly be, and it causes my belly to flip a little. "I might not like hearing it, Bodie, but if you're worried about the baby in any way as we proceed along, you need to be vocal."

"I will," I promise. Why she even needs to tell me this is beyond me, because nothing could keep me silent if my kid was at risk.

This seems to satisfy her, and she gives a grateful nod. That unsettles me... that she seems to need me to be a checks and balances against her. It also reassures me that when Rachel said she was going to let me be involved, she truly meant it.

More than anything, though, it shows me she cares for this baby at least to the degree she wants to carry it to term. An adrenaline junkie such as herself who doesn't want to be pregnant wouldn't think twice about risks. That person would roll the dice with a *que sera sera* attitude.

There are a million ways I could poke at this more, but I don't want to do anything to make Rachel clam up on me. Right now, she's happy to let me fuck her and be involved in this pregnancy. I know a good thing when I have it.

But the one thing that has happened since finding out about the pregnancy is that I've become infinitely more curious about this woman. She's smart, beautiful, and sexy as sin. She's also one of the most capable people I know, and I trust her with my life. She has agreed to carry a baby for me, and I owe her the world because of that. It's safe to say Rachel Hart has gone to the top of my favorite people list.

And I want to know more about her.

I roll to my back and bring Rachel with me. She gasps in surprise, but doesn't fight when I arrange her body to lay mostly on top of mine. I even put a hand to the back of her head and force it to my chest. It takes her a slight moment to understand what I want, but she eventually settles down on top of me.

"Okay, you have to tell me how a woman goes from being a winter Olympian to traveling around the world jumping off cliffs?"

Her body shakes slightly against me in a silent laugh. I'm not sure if she's even aware she's doing it, but her hand spreads over my chest, her thumb idly stroking my skin there.

"My parents are well off, and when I say well off, I mean I don't have to work if I don't want to because of a nice trust fund. But I had some endorsements during my Olympic career, which meant I had enough money to indulge in those whims. I didn't travel extravagantly, but I did travel the hell out of this world. I'd often just sleep in cheap hotels or stay with friends. I once spent two weeks driving around Australia in an old VW bus that doubled as a bed for me."

"It sounds very bohemian of you," I observe.

"I was young and liked the freedom," she says. "I'd never had to think about what I wanted to be when I grew up. I'd been training since I was a kid for the biathlon. When I finally got tired of it, I had no idea what to do with myself."

"You deserved a break," I point out.

"Yes, that's the way I reasoned it out in my head. But a few weeks turned into months and that turned into years. I chased thrills and lived like a bum for four years."

"Sounds kind of cool," I admit a little wistfully. It's very different from my life of responsibility, whether it was working on the farm since I was probably ten to going right into the Navy after high school. I'd always had obligations I'd never walk away from.

Maybe that's why I feel so strongly about this baby... while Rachel is sort of able to treat it like a road bump in her life.

CHAPTER 8

Rachel

I NORMALLY LOVE the sounds of a gym. Clanging of metal on metal, the hum of a treadmill, and the grunts of exertion. It's certainly no chore when the gym is busy such as it is now with hot, ripped guys. I've never been able to explain the phenomena, but for some reason, men have to be insanely gorgeous and built to perfection to work at The Jameson Group. My eyes are having a tough time staying focused on my little work area because I keep wanting to let them stray over to Bodie while he works out with Cage. We'd all flown in on a private charter from L.A. this morning, and then we shared an Uber to come right to the gym to workout.

It was slightly weird flying back with the team, and by weird, I mean sitting across from Bodie and not continually thinking about how great sex is with him. He and I stayed up a good chunk of the night and into the early morning hours just gorging on each other. I kicked him out of my bed around three AM, so I could get a few hours of sleep before our flight. He grumbled about it, but he eventually went. Whenever I happened to look at him during the flight, he would either shoot me a wink or knowing smile. One time, he even licked his bottom lip. I almost combusted.

Damn pregnancy hormones.

The Jameson Group's gym is state of the art and geared for more than just strength or cardio training. A huge rock wall takes up the eastern side, extending up two stories. There's an indoor obstacle course that would rival any military boot camp facility, and just off the gym complex is an indoor shooting range. My favorite, though, is the knife station. Three straw dummies are set up with head, chest, and femoral artery targets, and there's a case full of different-sized throwing knives.

I'm practicing trying to hit the femoral artery of the dummy that's furthest away. So far, I've managed to hit his little straw nuts three times in a row. I pick up a six-inch Japanese Shinobi, flip it in the air so I catch it by the blade, and cock my arm back to launch. Clearing my mind, I focus my gaze to the left side of the dummy's nut sack and let my confidence clear the way. I launch, and the silver knife glints as it tumbles end over end.

Solid strike to the testicles once again.

"Goddamn motherfucking hairy balls," I growl a little too loudly. Tank Richardson, another explosives expert at Jameson, gives me a startled look as he throws knives at the dummy in the lane next to me.

"Sorry," I mutter.

"Take a deep breath," he says as he chooses a knife from the tray beside him.

"Excuse me?" I snap. I don't need to be told to calm the fuck down, which given the quick flush of anger that overtakes me, might actually be good advice.

Fuck you, pregnancy hormones.

"It helps if just before you throw, you take a deep breath and hold it," he says, either unaware of the anger brewing just under the surface or not really caring.

Knowing Tank, he just doesn't care. He's a big brute of a guy with the personality of a fresh Brillo pad. All abrasive and uncaring if he scratches people up.

"Thanks for nothing," I mutter under my breath. Tank throws his knife, and it hits the dummy's right eye. He gives me a knowing smirk, and I contemplate launching my next knife to see if I can hit that curve of his lip on the left side of his face.

Even though I can't stand him in this moment, I grudgingly accept Tank's advice and suck in a deep breath. I cock my arm, take aim, and laser my eyes onto the target.

Launch.

Strike.

Direct hit to the testicles yet again.

Fury at my own ineptitude paralyzes me for a moment. It's how I felt when I saw Joram take a bullet, and then an image of Tank smirking at me fills my gaze. He's not actually smirking at me right now because I'm still staring at the knife lodged firmly in the center of the dummy's groin, but I can just imagine it.

The paralyzed feeling melts away, and I'm able to move. In a burst of frustration, my hand flies out, sweeping the entire knife case off the table beside me. It goes flying a good ten feet before the knives clatter out against the concrete flooring.

"You stupid motherfucking useless testicle-guided butter knives," I yell at my adversaries, cringing when the echo of my own petulant tantrum is thrown back at me.

There's immediate silence in the gym, as if every single person stopped what they were doing to look my way. My head drops, and I stare at my tennis shoes for a moment before I get up the courage to look over at Tank. He's staring at me with his jaw dropped.

Tears spring to my eyes, and I'm horrified when they start to spill over my bottom lids. Tank's eyebrows disappear into his military-style buzz cut, but I only see that for a blessedly brief moment before his entire face becomes hazy through the water in my eyes.

"Fuck," I mutter and spin away from Tank and the knives. I dart across a small area set up with a squat rack where Sal Mezzina and Benji Darden are working out. As I jog past, wiping my eyes with the back of my hand, Sal calls in his thick Bronx accent, "Hey Hart... what are the tears for? On the rag or something?"

It's not the first period joke I've heard from my male

coworkers, and it's never bothered me before. But apparently, my hormones were in a state of dormancy prior to getting knocked up, and a fresh wave of tears well in my eyes.

Another wave of pure rage rockets through me, heating me up from the inside out. I swear I can even feel my earlobes sizzling.

I veer left and change course without thinking, barreling right at Sal. Through the tears and fury, I see his eyes grow wide. He opens his mouth and holds his hands up in slow motion as if to stop me, but my hands slam right into his chest and he goes flying. Right through the back of the squat rack and onto his ass with a resounding thud.

I come to stand over the top of him, legs spread wide and hands on my hips.

"I've got your rag for you, you fucking sexist pig," I scream.

He stares up at me as if I have horns sprouting from the top of my head. The way I feel right this moment, it wouldn't surprise me to find them there. My body is not my own.

This enrages me further and I open my mouth to lay every vile curse word in my arsenal on him, when an arm circles me from behind.

Because I know his body so well, I recognize the planes and contours of Bodie's chest as I'm hauled backward into it.

I'm offended he'd think to stop me in the middle of my tirade; especially since, as a woman being shamed for her period, I have a right to be incensed. Doesn't matter that it has never bothered me before, or that I've always taken it as the type of ribbing from male teammates that means I'm part of their inner circle of trust.

"Easy does it, Hart," Bodie murmurs in my ear in an attempt to calm me, but I'm thinking that would require some serious anti-psychotic medication at this point.

"Fuck you, Bodie," I yell as I wrench out of his grasp. Well, he actually lets me go quite easily, and that he knows just what my boundaries are pisses me off even more.

Bodie stares at me warily, face etched with concern. He doesn't spare a glance at Sal still sitting on the floor.

I think it might even be okay... that I can come out of this without any embarrassment, but those stupid fucking tears start again, sliding down my cheeks in frustratingly itchy rivulets. Bodie's expression goes from worried to pitying, and it's the straw that breaks this pregnant psycho's back.

"Fuck you," I snarl at Bodie before looking at Sal again. "And fuck you. Don't ever say something like that to me again."

Sal gives me a tight nod, but I don't give a fuck if he agrees with my right to claim a harassment-free environment. He's already forgotten as I spin on my heel and barrel through the glass door that leads into the coed locker room.

I stomp across to my locker, and I'm so furious I can't get my combo entered correctly. On the second attempt, I'm cursing.

On the third, I'm crying harder.

"Rachel…" My body locks tight at the sound of Bodie's voice behind me. "What's wrong?"

I ignore him, take a deep breath, and try the combo again.

Bingo. It fucking works. Hallelujah. Something is going right in my life.

"You know Sal was just kidding with you, right?" he says.

I spin on him, incredulously glaring at his insensitivity. And I see it on his face as clear as day. He knows that's a stupid remark to make to a hormonal pregnant female who was just teased about something that makes her distinctly female in a heavily male-dominated working environment.

He said it specifically to provoke me into conversation, even at the risk of inciting more fury from me.

I can't help it. I just break.

Right in half.

More tears come pouring out, and my chest tightens with anxiety that I'm having this meltdown.

At work.

In front of Bodie.

"I'm a fucking mess," I wail loudly, and then my face

is mashed into Bodie's sweaty chest because his arms are around me. I take in a deep breath, appreciate the male sweat along with his strength for just a moment, and then pull my head back so I can speak. "My knife-throwing skills are for shit. I can only hit the nut sack, and that will put my teammates in jeopardy. Sure, a knife to the balls will drop someone, but it's not a kill shot and sometimes I'll need a kill shot. And Sal... he's a douche. And I think he's on steroids, which makes him a bigger douche, and he has no fucking right to talk about my period, which I no longer have because I'm pregnant. Knocked up. I'm going to get fat, and it's going to fucking hurt so bad when I give birth. And Bodie... did you know that these hormones cause zits? I'm breaking out on my chin, and I haven't had fucking acne since I was sixteen and—"

My face is mashed back into his chest with his big hand cupping my head. I feel his lips press to the top of my head, and he rocks me slightly back and forth. For a glorious few minutes, I accept his strength. I burrow into him and revel in the cocoon of his arms wrapped around me. My tears dry up, and my chest loosens slightly.

But that moment of respite fades as I take in the sounds around me. Lockers being closed, and the dull murmur of voices.

My head snaps up, and I push slightly away from Bodie to look around. There are three other people here in various stages of undress. Ice prickles down my spine as I realize... Bodie hadn't wrapped me in a tight hug with my face pressed to his chest to comfort me. He'd tried to stop my tirade, which had included bemoaning the fact I'm pregnant even though it was supposed to be a secret.

"Jesus Christ," I murmur, and my head drops in shame over my own stupidity. Tears form in my eyes again when I realize the cat is out of the bag, and I feel tremendously sorry for myself. That thin thread of control I had regained from Bodie's strength is starting to slip, and I'm afraid I might scream in frustration.

My body tightens up defensively, waiting for Bodie to offer me solace again. If he does, I think it might break me completely.

Instead, I jolt and my head jerks up to look at him in surprise when he says, "You need to suck it up, Hart."

His voice is low.

Calm.

Assured.

His expression is neutral without any condemnation over my tantrum.

"Excuse me?" I say through the hoarse buildup of emotion in my throat. My eyes dry up like a sponge was pressed to the corners.

"Suck up the taunts from guys like Sal," he says in a commanding tone that's still so low only I can hear it. "If you can't suck it up, stay away from the locker room and gym until your hormones cool down. Or come to me.

You can let it out on me. At the very least, I'll fuck it out of you."

Many women would be offended by his blasé, cold attitude. But honestly... it's exactly what I needed to reorient myself.

If Bodie had touched me in sympathy or tried to comfort me again, I'd have probably gone ape shit.

He knew.

He absolutely fucking knew what I needed. I needed him to tell me to be strong. Just before that, I needed him to hug me, and he knew that, too.

He gave me what I needed both times without me even asking for it.

Bodie's fingers come under my chin, forcing me to look up at him. He steps in just slightly and murmurs, "You come to me. You got it?"

I give him a slight nod.

"I've got your back, Rachel," he says softly. "Always."

I want to cry again, but I don't.

Instead, I marvel at something that's uncurling from deep within my chest.

Never once since I fucked Bodie or found out I was pregnant had I ever considered developing feelings for him. I saw this as an arrangement. A way for me to take responsibility for my poor choices when it came to safe sex.

It never occurred to me that Bodie could provoke something inside of me.

But those words.

I've got your back, Rachel. Always.

I have no clue what Bodie is to me, but he is most definitely not just a sperm donor or casual fuck anymore.

CHAPTER 9

Bodie

*"**O**LSON MANAGES TO get a stick on the puck, kicks it out, and Fabritis pulls it free. Across to Samuelson and… he scores! Garrett Samuelson over the right shoulder of Bertrand to put the Cold Fury up four to two."*

"Goal," Cage yells, throwing his hands up in victory as the hockey players on TV are all hugs and backslaps. "That fucking Stanley Cup is ours again this year."

I laugh and shake my head. Cage is from North Carolina and sort of psycho for his Carolina Cold Fury. He went to every game of the Stanley Cup finals last year where they won. I expect he'll do the same this year if they make it past this round of the playoffs.

As for hockey, not my thing. Growing up in the Midwest, it was all about football. Cornhusker football to be exact. One of the things I miss most about my dad is watching college football on Saturday's together. I expect if I head home with a baby that tradition will be in place once again, which is a good thing.

"Another beer, Bodie?" the bartender asks, and I nod.

"Me too," Cage says before he picks up his pint glass and drains the rest. I'd gladly said yes when he invited me out for a late lunch and some beers while he watched the hockey game on TV. We're at our favorite sports bar in Vegas, and we're well known here.

The bartender snags our empties and discards them into a sink behind the bar. She grabs two more chilled glasses from a cooler and pours our drafts.

The hockey game cuts away to a commercial for a sports drink, and our fresh beers are slid in front of us. Just as I pick mine up to take a sip, Cage says, "So Hart's pregnant, huh?"

My glass freezes halfway to my mouth for just a second before I regain my senses. I take a large mouthful and then set the pint glass on the counter, carefully calculating my response. Clearly her meltdown in the locker room has made the gossip rounds.

"Yeah," I say, turning to look at him. "She was just having a rough day, I guess."

"That's wild," Cage says thoughtfully. "Thinking about Hart being pregnant, that is. I can't think of a woman who is less motherly than her."

It shouldn't bother me... those words.

But they do.

They bother me because he's right. Rachel has made it clear she doesn't want to be a mom at this point in her life. But he's also wrong. She's also wrong.

I can see the potential within her.

"I wonder if Kynan knocked her up," he muses before taking a sip of his beer.

"Why would you say that?" I ask. It comes out a little too aggressively.

Cage turns his head to look me in the eye. "Oh, come on. They've got a past. Fuck buddies and all that."

My abdomen contracts painfully, like I'd been kicked right in the gut. The news is jarring.

"They're fuck buddies?" I ask, my throat dry. I'm not sure why it bothers me, because what she did in her past shouldn't matter.

Not really.

I've watched her fuck random men at The Wicked Horse, and that's never bothered me. Still doesn't, as a matter of fact, because I know it was meaningless.

Just like the women I've fucked there were meaningless.

But Kynan?

That's not meaningless. They've known each other a long fucking time. Since before The Jameson Group.

"How do you know they're fuck buddies?" I ask, trying to appear casual about my inquiry.

Cage shrugs. "Well, it's just rumor really. Some of the original members like Sal and Tank were talking about it in the locker room earlier today. Said they were an item back in the day."

After Rachel had her public meltdown and then

jetted out of there. It took no more than a few minutes before all the guys were gossiping like a bunch of clucking hens.

And what the fuck does "back in the day" even mean?

I pick up my beer and start chugging. I'd like Rachel to clear up those matters for me. Otherwise, I'll drive myself batty wondering about it. Right now, she's fucking me exclusively, but I need to know if she's got feelings for Kynan. I respect the dude, and I respect Rachel. I don't want to stand in the way of something.

I also don't want to have these nasty-ass feelings I've got going on right now, which are ranging from jealousy to anger.

"It's got to be Kynan, right?" Cage chatters on. I continue swallowing large mouthfuls of beer. "I mean… they've got a history, and Hart's not the type to have unprotected sex. If it happened, it was planned is the way I'm thinking. Kynan's got to be the dad for sure—"

"It's mine," I croak after swallowing the last of my beer, sucking air through my teeth. I slam my glass on the bar, and turn to lock my eyes to Cage's.

His eyes go round, his mouth dropping wide open. "Yours?"

"Mine," I say proprietarily, and I wonder if that's for the baby, Rachel, or both. I wait for a flash of guilt to hit me that I've divulged our secret. Rachel most certainly didn't want anyone to know she's pregnant just yet. She didn't want to be treated differently by the guys, but that cat is out of the bag thanks to her hormonal rant earlier today.

She also doesn't want anyone to know we're involved, and I get that, too. It's an unspoken rule, and it will make things awkward. Since I've been with Jameson, there's never been a romantic or sexual relationship between members. Or at least not out in the open anyway.

But Cage is my best friend, and I wanted him to stop talking about Kynan and her being together. It was getting on my nerves.

"What the fuck?" Cage growls in a low voice. "You and Hart? Together?"

"Well, we're not together-together," I hedge as I push my empty glass to the edge. The bartender starts my way, but I shake my head, indicating I don't want another. "But things got carried away between us in Paphos, and she got pregnant."

"What… break a condom?"

"Didn't use a condom," I mutter.

"You fucking idiot," Cage says. I couldn't agree with him more, but what's done is done. Now we have to accept the consequences. "But what do you mean you're not together-together? That means you're together in some way?"

"We're fucking." My words are pointed and clear. They shouldn't invite other questions, but I still add,

"Exclusively."

"Lucky son of a bitch." Cage shakes his head disbelievingly. "She's pretty much every man's fantasy."

"Yeah, well stop thinking about her that way." I cringe over the possessive snarl in my tone, but it's better than peeing in a circle around Rachel. That would just be embarrassing.

As if it just hits Cage with the implications of everything he's learned, he leans toward me and asks in a low, hesitant voice. "Are y'all going to get married or something?"

That makes me smile, because it just never crosses Cage's mind to ask if we're keeping the baby. He's my closest friend in the world, the bond forged tight by the many hair-raising adventures we've shared in the Navy and with the Jameson Group. He knows I would never consider *not* having this kid.

I also know I need to tell him the truth because I can't lie to him. But I also trust him to keep this confidential.

Leaning against the back of the barstool, I scrub my hands over my face. When I look back at him, my words start on an exhale. "Rachel doesn't want the baby, but I do. She's agreed to carry it, and I'm going to raise it."

Cage just stares at me, blinking a few times as he reconciles the fucked-up dichotomy of my relationship with Rachel. The total reversal of stereotyped roles where the mother doesn't want the baby, but the father does.

"How?" Cage demands angrily. "How are you going to raise a kid on your own?"

"You know how," I say softly, acknowledging the heaviness in my heart that I'll be giving up a career I love in exchange. "The baby has to be my first priority. Over everything."

"You'll go home to Nebraska," Cage says in realization, his voice as heavy sounding as my heart is feeling. "Estelle and Geo will go crazy over another grandkid."

That's the truth. Cage knows my parents well since he's been a guest at the Wright household many times over the years. He has no family of his own, so my mom and dad have unofficially adopted him.

"You know I can't have this career and handle a kid on my own. There's just no way."

"And no chance Hart will change her mind?" he asks. "The two of you could do it together."

"I have no clue," I tell my best friend, and then look over to the bartender. I lift my hand and point to the empty, indicating I've changed my mind about the beer. There's still two more periods to the hockey game, and while I really don't care to finish watching it, Cage will. I might as well get a good buzz going as that might make things at least feel a little better.

The bartender nabs my empty, dumps it in the sink, and pours me a fresh beer.

"You care for her," Cage says out of the blue when I pick the beer up for a sip. His tone is a mix of accusation and wonder. "I watched you run out of the gym after her this morning. You were hugging her in the locker room—according to the reports I heard. More importantly, Hart was letting you comfort her, and we all know that's very anti-Hart. You two care for each other."

My head is shaking in denial before he can even finish. "It's not like that."

"Bullshit," he declares.

"Okay, yes... I care about her," I admit. "I mean, man... she's giving up part of her life for me. I'm asking her to put her body through hell to give birth to a baby. For me. I'm asking her to do something monumental for me, so yes... I care about her. How could I not?"

"She cares about you, too," Cage proclaims with a sharp nod of his head.

"As a teammate," I finish his thought. "She's doing this because of team loyalty and respect. Nothing more."

Cage nods, not necessarily in agreement, but more so that the depth or origin of her care is probably irrelevant. She's committed to carrying the baby, and that speaks volumes either way.

"Listen, buddy..." Cage picks his beer up and holds it up to me in a toast. "I know this isn't how you envisioned becoming a father would happen. I know you thought your family would be built in a more traditional way. But congrats. You're going to make a fucking awesome dad, and I'm thoroughly depressed you're going to be leaving me."

I laugh and pick up my beer. After I tap it against his, we drink deeply. I fucking don't want to leave, but I see no other option at this point.

Cage sets his beer down, his eyes drifting to the TV mounted on the wall behind the bar. His attention isn't fully focused on it, because he still has questions about Rachel. "I assume all this is on the down low?"

"Yeah," I say, my eyes on the hockey game, too, my fingers playing mindlessly in the condensation on the pint glass. "Obviously the pregnancy is out in the open, but no one knows it's mine."

"Lips are sealed," he says, but he doesn't need to do that. I know they are.

"Appreciate it."

"And if you need to talk, I'm here."

"I know," I say softly. I can envision plenty of beers with Cage before all this is said and done, because as we advance through the months, it's only going to get tougher.

At some point, it will come out that I'm the daddy. At some point, I'll need to tell my parents. And at some point, I'll need to make plans to leave Jameson.

At some point.

But not tonight.

Tonight, I'm drinking beer with my buddy, and I'm thinking I ought to just get shit faced. It's been a while since I've done it. What better reason to do so than the fact my life is getting ready to be turned upside down?

My phone gives off a short vibration, indicating an incoming text. I pull it out and see it's from Rachel.

Meet me at The Wicked Horse at 11pm.

I stare at the message for what seems like forever. So long that Cage leans over to see what I'm looking at, but I turn the screen away from him.

Our one encounter in The Wicked Horse was impulsive and dangerous. If we want to keep our sexual relationship a secret, there can't be any fucking around there.

Still, I type my response back without worrying about repercussions. *Ok. CU then.*

That's still several hours away, and I've got some beers still to drink. But I won't drink too many. I want to keep my wits about me when dealing with Rachel.

CHAPTER 10

Rachel

I SIT BACK casually on the small velvet couch in The Apartment. I don't see any other Jameson employees in here other than Kynan, who is playing poker right now. Not everyone at Jameson has a membership to The Wicked Horse. Not even most of them, actually. Just those who are into kinky fucking in a public manner.

The Apartment is fairly dead tonight. Maybe because it's a Sunday night and the workweek is starting in a few hours. There's a rambunctious game of poker going on, and I listen in because Kynan is in a taunting mood and that amuses me.

"Interested in a side bet?" he asks the only woman playing with the group of men. She reminds me of a slightly older version of Taylor Swift. Sweet face set off by a blunt cut of blonde bangs across her forehead.

"Like what?" she asks with her head tilted to the side.

"I win, you come over here and give me a blow job. You win, I'll make you come with my mouth."

I snicker but truly, I expected no different than Kynan betting body parts.

The woman doesn't even get a chance to respond because a smokin' hot guy sitting next to her says, "Not going to happen."

"I can answer for myself," the woman retorts, but she turns to smile at the guy who is now staring daggers at Kynan.

He finally turns his gaze to the blonde woman, but he sweeps his hand toward Kynan. "Go ahead. But he already got the message."

"I like it when you go all Neanderthal on me," the woman purrs, and I think… that's actually kind of sweet.

The hot guy finds it hilarious, because he gives a hearty laugh. "In that case, I'll make sure to pull your hair hard when I fuck you later."

Okay, that's just hot. I can imagine Bodie doing that to me, and it makes me squirm in my seat. I glance at my watch. He should be arriving soon. I'm not sure what I want to do with him or where, but I do know I want to do something.

Laughter at the poker table has me tuning back in, and I see the woman raking in the poker chips. She must have won whatever bet was made when I tuned them out.

Everyone stands from the table, one guy heading off toward the restroom and another arching his back. They're clearly going to take a bit of a break.

Kynan stands there, talking to one of the other players while he sips on a whiskey. His gaze cuts over to the Taylor Swift lookalike and the hot guy.

I do the same, continuing to stare as she crawls onto his lap. Within moments, they're fucking right there at the table. Kynan keeps his gaze pinned on the couple while he talks, but he's visibly aroused. His erection is pressed thick and long against his dress pants.

There was a day that would have made my mouth water, but I don't think like that about him anymore. All I seem to think about is Bodie's cock and the way it makes me feel.

The woman rides her man's dick, and the sight is turning me on. I wish Bodie would get here.

Kynan comes to sit down next to me on the couch and I'm momentarily startled because I'd been staring so intently at the couple fucking right there at the poker table. Kynan adjusts his dick slightly before crossing one leg over the other.

"What are you doing here tonight, Rachel?" he asks as he slings an arm over the back of the couch, his fingers brushing against my shoulder.

"Going to get laid if Bodie will ever get here," I say nonchalantly, checking my watch again.

"Damn," Kynan says in a low, appreciative voice.

My head snaps to the side, and I look at him questioningly. "What?"

"You're going public, huh?"

I give a little sniff followed by a shrug. "Why hide it?"

"Why indeed?" he agrees. I bristle over the slight taunt in his voice, not liking that he finds me amusing. But then his voice drops even lower, and he's no longer amused but worried instead. "I heard you had a bit of a hard time at the gym today."

"Ugh," I say with a huff and lean back into the couch cushion. "Stupid fucking hormones. I was a total girl today. Boohooing like a baby."

"Everyone knows you're pregnant now," he says, but I already knew that.

"Well, it was going to come out eventually," I say glumly. "Might as well hit it head on."

"You're going to have some people questioning your ability," he points out.

"I'm pregnant," I snap. "Not disabled."

"I know that. Others will know that. Some won't. You're going to need to set the record straight, Rachel."

"Fine," I say with a sigh, and then look at my watch again.

"Your prince arrives," Kynan says softly.

My head pops up, immediately locking eyes with Bodie as he walks my way. He's all in black tonight. Black jeans, black biker boots, and a heavy black leather jacket over a black Harley Davidson t-shirt that I can see peeking through at his very well-formed chest. I press my legs together in anticipation.

My gaze travels back up his body, and I'm surprised to find him staring daggers at Kynan. I stand up from the couch and take a few steps toward Bodie. When he reaches me, he looks down at me with an uneasy expression on his face and a clenched jaw.

"Are you and Kynan fucking each other?" he asks me ever so softly and so no one else can hear his ludicrous question except for me.

"Why would you ask that?"

He rubs his neck in what appears to be frustration. "Because it would seem that's the prevalent thought among all the people who are gossiping about your pregnancy."

I want to be angry he's asking me something so personal, but damn it all to hell, I find it endearing. "I'm not fucking Kynan."

"Have you ever?" he asks so suddenly that I know he's been told I have. More gossip, I assume, but this time it's accurate.

"Many years ago," I tell him truthfully. "Before I came to work for Jameson."

His eyes leave mine, traveling over my shoulder. I look behind me, but Kynan is gone from the couch. I twist my head a little further and see him back at the poker table, ignoring us.

When I turn back to Bodie, I see him staring at Kynan with a furrowed brow. I bring my hand to his face, and he flinches minutely before looking at me.

"You're the only one I'm fucking now." I take satisfaction in the slight flare of lust in his eyes. "In fact, I'd very much like for us to fuck tonight."

"Is anyone else here from Jameson?" he asks, his words thick and heavy with need as he looks around The Apartment.

"Doesn't matter," I say, and his gaze crashes back into mine with disbelief. "I don't care if anyone knows. Cat's out of the bag about the pregnancy, so why hide that we're fucking each other?"

He winces slightly at the reminder that what we're doing is nothing but sex, and I wonder if that means he views it as something more. I refuse to let myself feel that way because that would only complicate things once the baby is born.

Bodie grabs my hand and starts to tug me toward the door. "Let's go to one of the other rooms."

"No," I say as I pull back, causing him to turn to face me.

I lace my fingers with his and walk back to the couch I'd been sitting on. I risk a glance over at Kynan and I see him watching us now with interest from over the cards he has in his hand.

Bodie doesn't fight me when I push him onto the gray velvet cushion. He spreads his legs slightly, and I step between them. Lifting his chin, he watches me with a thoughtfulness that tells me he's intrigued.

I drop to my knees and bring my hands to his thighs.

His muscles contract under my touch before relaxing again. The connection between us seems to crackle. My hands tremble slightly as I slide my palms up, moving them inward to graze over his erection.

"I don't care if anyone watches us," I tell him softly as my fingers work at the button to his jeans. I hope he understands the understatement within my words.

I don't care if Kynan watches us because Kynan is nothing to me other than a friend.

Bodie's teeth dig down into his bottom lip while I slide the zipper down slowly. He lifts his hips slightly as I peel the fly open, digging in to pull his cock out.

It's thick and solid. I drag my thumb up the vein on the underside before wrapping my hand around its warmth, squeezing tightly. Bodie groans and lifts his hips again.

"This is mine," I whisper as I stare up at him. "And I'm hungry."

"Fuck, Rachel," he practically wheezes with need.

I'd never make him wait, so I lean over and take him in my mouth. His skin feels hotter on my tongue, my jaws stretching to accommodate his size. Images of him fucking my mouth spring to mind. I know if he ever let loose on me, I'd easily choke on his cock. That thought soaks my panties.

But that is for another night of play. We have so much to learn about and try with each other, and The Wicked Horse will be our sinful playground for months to come.

Or, at least, until I really start showing and then I'm not about to flash my pregnant belly to anyone but Bodie. Dr. Anchors assured me that sex—even vigorous sex—was perfectly fine, and I've watched Bodie at times here in the club.

The man has a deviously filthy mind, and I'm going to enjoy every fucking second of what he can do to me.

I grip his shaft at the base, giving short, tight strokes as I suck and lick on him. The sounds he makes are tortured, and his pre-cum tastes deliciously salty. He's going to taste even better going down my throat.

Bodie's hands come to my head, cradling me softly. "Slow down."

I can't talk with a mouth full of his gorgeous cock, so I give a short shake to my head before I suck him in extra deep.

"Fuck," he mutters, lifting his hips again to push the tip into my throat. I swallow, feeling myself contract around him, and he gives a tiny bark of surprise.

Before I can even acknowledge the triumph of making him feel amazing with that little trick, he's pushing me off his cock and my mouth is empty.

"What the hell—"

My words are cut off as I'm somehow lifted and spun around, landing on my hands and knees on the couch. Bodie roughly pushes my dress over my ass, jerks the crotch of my panties aside so the elastic bites into my skin, and presses two fingers into me.

My back dips in a deep arch, and I groan from the invasion. It's perfect.

"Wet for me, babe," he murmurs. He settles just one knee down into the cushion behind me, his other leg stretched out and foot planted on the floor. His fingers are gone, and then the fat, thick head of his cock is pushing into me.

My eyes flutter closed, but spring open in shock and utter fulfillment as he thrusts deep into me and then sets a fast pace. When the haze of pleasure clears, I realize we're facing directly at Kynan, who is watching us while he plays poker.

Dropping my gaze down to the velvet beneath me, I hide the slight smile that comes to my mouth. I don't even have to look over my shoulder at Bodie while he fucks me doggie style. I can guarantee he's staking his territory to Kynan whether I'm currently fucking him or not. I suspect he'd be staring down anyone in the Jameson Group if they were here right now, letting everyone know that my cunt is his.

Bodie's hands circle my waist, pulling me against him as he rides me.

Rides me hard and fast. My orgasm bursts outward in a glorious shower of pleasure that ripples through my body. I cry out from the perfect feeling, tiny shudders dancing up my spine when Bodie slams deep and groans out his release inside of me.

"Fucking perfect," he whispers as he starts to move again, tiny thrusts to prolong the tremors of a fading orgasm.

My head lifts, and I look at Kynan. He's got his head bowed over his cards, but there's no mistaking the amused smile on his face.

I twist my neck, looking at Bodie, who is grinning at me triumphantly.

"Proud of yourself?" I ask with a smirk.

"Yup," he says, smoothing his hand over my ass. He squeezes and then pulls out. "Let me catch my breath, and then I want to go fuck in The Waterfall Room."

"The Waterfall Room?" My interest is definitely piqued.

Bodie gently sets the crotch of my panties to right and lowers my dress over my ass. I rise from the couch and turn to face him.

With a hand to the back of my neck, he bends down to give me a kiss. It's our first of the evening. When he pulls back, his eyes are dancing with wickedness. "I want to fuck your tits under the waterfall. Then your mouth. Want to feel that little throat thing you did on me again."

"Dirty man," I murmur appreciatively. I hope it doesn't take him long to recharge because I'm ready to go again.

Right now.

I know my hormones are out of whack, and I'm

definitely hornier than normal. The thing is, I really don't know if it's the hormones or Bodie, because I only feel this way when I'm in proximity to him.

Strange.

Bodie's eyes slide past me to Kynan, and he gives a little wink and nod of his head. I don't even bother to look at Kynan because I already know the expression that will be on his face.

Amused.

He'll definitely be amused.

CHAPTER 11

Bodie

SOMEONE PUSHES A beer in my hand as I make my way through the crowd. I turn to see Hannah Miles standing next to a cooler filled with ice and long necks.

"Thanks, Hannah banana," I say with a grin. "Where's Steven?"

She rolls her eyes. "At the casino. Where else?"

My smile turns sympathetic. Hannah's a woman who doesn't get much satisfaction at home. Much like Rachel, she's married to her job. The difference between the two women is Hannah does it for financial security to support her family and her husband's gambling habits. Rachel does it because she loves it.

"Bodie," someone calls from across the crowd. I look up and glance around, locating Cage standing near the door that leads onto Kynan's back patio.

He's throwing a sort of "employee appreciation" party which he does periodically. Our crew at Jameson functions a lot like a family. By the nature of our work, we have to have the utmost respect and trust in each other. That doesn't mean we have to all like each other personally, but we do have to have enough of a bond that we can depend on each other when the going gets tough. Kynan likes to foster that by bringing us together as a group every so often.

It's nothing fancy. Usually just beer and burgers at his house, but it is a good way for us to relax and connect with each other. Add in employee spouses or partners, and there are easily a hundred people here today. That's not even counting everyone since some teams are out on missions.

Winding my way over to Cage, I find him talking to Locke and Benji.

"What's up?" I say as I reach the guys.

"Not much," Locke says in return. "Are you geared up for next week?"

"Ready as I'll ever be," I say as I twist the cap off my beer and pocket it. Truth be told, I'm ready for a little adventure.

Next week, a team of seven—myself and Rachel included—are headed to Singapore where we'll provide temporary security for a diesel tanker traveling through the Strait of Malacca. Somali piracy is so yesterday. Today's new and improved pirate targets diesel-laden cargo ships while they travel through choke points. Rather than take the crew of a ship hostage for ransom, they merely overpower and subdue so they can siphon off the gas, which fetches upward of half a million dollars on the black market for one good score. Merchant ships have taken to hiring private security groups to escort them through the choke points. We'll fly into Singapore, board the ship, and travel with it through the strait to ensure its safety.

"So," Benji drawls in a lowered voice after he steps in closer to me. "Is it true? Hart's pregnant? We've asked Cage, but he's playing all stupid."

I can't help but bristle against his nosiness, even though I know the record needs to be set straight. I'm sure Rachel's little meltdown and admission in the locker room that's she's pregnant has made all the rounds, and every single person in this house knows about it.

But that's Rachel's story to tell how she sees fit. I've only told Cage—and I let Rachel know I did—and that's the way I'm keeping it.

Before I can even brush Benji off, Locke elbows him in the ribs and nods at something behind me. "Ask her yourself."

I turn around to see Rachel talking to Hannah, clutching a bottle of water in her hands. She's got her hair pulled back in that short ponytail, which is nothing but about two inches of hair hanging out the end. Locks have fallen loose and frame her pretty face, making her look young and fresh. She's wearing a pair of frayed denim shorts, a loose tank top, and flat sandals. She's dressed the part for a late spring cookout.

As if she can sense my stare, she turns slightly away from Hannah and locks her eyes with mine. Even though we've spent every night together since that amazing one at The Wicked Horse almost a week ago, I can't really say we're dating. Otherwise, we would have come to the cookout together.

Instead, I woke up in my bed this morning with her mouth on my cock. The woman loves to suck my dick, and I love her doing it. I let her this time, barely controlling myself from pouncing and fucking her. She swallowed me down when I came and then gave me a hard kiss before she rolled out of bed. I had thought briefly about asking her if she wanted to ride together today, but I hadn't.

I knew the answer would be "no".

Rachel has set the boundaries. We can stay the night at each other's house or we can fuck in The Wicked Horse. We haven't been back to the club since the night I staked my claim on her while Kynan watched me fuck her. That was awesome in and of itself, and I'm sure we'll go back. It's just that each night this week, she's shown up at my house a little after dinner and I gladly let her in.

Rachel turns and says something else to Hannah, but then she's heading my way. Her eyes flit from me to Cage to Locke to Benji, then back to me again by the time she reaches us.

"What's up?" she asks, the same casual question Locke asked me when I walked up.

No one says a word. Benji and Locke just stare at her, hoping perhaps she'll blurt out the details of what's going on with her. Cage sips his beer, watching with amusement.

I save the awkwardness by saying, "I just got here. Haven't even seen Kynan yet."

"He's probably out manning the grill," she surmises as she takes a sip of her bottled water. Benji and Locke watch her intently, as if the fact she's drinking water confirms she's knocked up.

Finally, Benji gets up the nerve to ask, "Want a beer, Hart? I'll go get you one."

"No thanks," she says with a pleasant smile, but I can tell by the tone in her voice she knows damn well why the question was asked.

"Wine?" Locke asks, adding, "There's red and white."

Rachel rolls her eyes. "Oh, for fuck's sake."

She turns her attention to me. "Is it going to be like this all day?"

"Probably," I say with a sympathetic wince. Cage snickers.

Rachel shoves her water bottle at me, and I almost bobble my beer making a grab for it. She puts a hand to my shoulder and uses me for leverage to climb on a chair I'm standing next to. Putting her fingers in her mouth, she lets fly a piercing shriek of a whistle, which cuts through all the chatter.

Total silence and all eyes are on Rachel.

"Thank you for your attention," she calls to the people standing around Kynan's living room, which spills into the kitchen. A few people come wandering in from the patio to check out what's going on. "As I'm sure you all have heard the gossip by now, I wanted to confirm that I am indeed pregnant. Eight weeks today as a matter of fact. So, you can all stop whispering about it and prodding me with sly questions that aren't all that sly. Is that clear?"

No one says a word.

"Good. A few other things you need to know. I have the doctor's clearance to continue to work for now. If any of you have an issue with me being pregnant, come talk to me privately. More importantly, because I know this is also being gossiped about… the baby is Bodie's. It was not planned, but we're dealing with it the best we can. Now, if no one has any questions, I'm fucking starved. Eating for two and all that. I'll be out near the grill getting a hamburger or four."

A smatter of laughs can be heard, but I'm just staring at Rachel in utter disbelief. I mean… good for her for taking the bull by the horns, but I wasn't expecting it.

Even more surprising is that her hands come to my shoulders before she steps off the chair. She looks me dead in the eye and asks, "Was that okay? I probably should have discussed that with you first."

"It was fine," I manage to say.

"Good," she says with a satisfied smile, and then I nearly fall over when she presses her mouth to mine. When she pulls back, she jumps off the chair and says, "I'm going to get something to eat. Want me to bring you something?"

I thrust my beer at Cage, who takes it without comment. Sweeping my hand toward the patio door, I tell her, "I'll come with you."

I mean... after that little public display of affection while everyone watched, why would I want to hang out with these dudes? I'd rather be by Rachel's side any day.

When we step out onto the patio, I immediately see Kynan manning the grill. He's got on a ridiculous apron that says, "May I Suggest the Sausage?" and has a hand with the finger pointed down toward his dick.

We walk that way. While I'm not touching Rachel in any way, many are looking at us speculatively. The people out here on the patio hadn't heard her big announcement, although I'm sure the news will make its way around quickly. Those who are looking now are the ones who saw me hugging her after she had her meltdown, and they are all wondering what the fuck is going on between us.

"I got burgers, brats, and hot dogs," Kynan says when we reach him. He waggles his eyebrows and points at his apron. "But the sausage is to die for."

Rachel rolls her eyes, and I'm pleased his childish reference to his dick doesn't bother me, knowing that said dick has touched Rachel. She said it was in the past. Several years in the past as a matter of fact.

Besides, she let me fuck her at the club right in front of Kynan, and I'm smart enough to know that was her way of proving to me that she was only into me.

Rachel turns to the long table set up beside the grill that has plates and toppings for the burgers, along with bowls of chips and various salads. She fixes herself a hamburger bun with globs of mustard. She then reaches into the bowl of potato chips and grabs a handful, crunching them down on top of the mustard-covered bun.

"That's interesting," I tease.

"Don't even start on me," she mutters as she picks up the plate and holds it out toward Kynan to put a burger on. "It's a craving thing apparently."

"Apparently," I say with a chuckle.

Kynan's eyes are shining with laughter, but I'm sure he likes his sausage where it is, so he silently scoops a burger off the grill with his spatula and slides it sizzling onto the pile of chips resting on the bun.

She licks her lower lip in anticipation, but as soon as she reaches to put the top of the bun on, she goes dead still. Her face pales, and she inhales sharply through her nose, which crinkles in distaste as soon as she does it. She shoves the plate so hard back at Kynan that it tips over and the mustard-soaked bun, burger, and chips splat against his chest.

"What the fuck?" Kynan growls as he looks down at his torso, but Rachel is slapping her hand over her mouth and reeling away. She stumbles several feet toward the edge of the patio, bends over with her arms crossing her stomach, and vomits into his landscaping right on top of a prickly cactus.

Without thought, I rush to Rachel's side and lay my hand on her lower back. She gags and retches for a few moments before she finally straightens up, rubbing at the side of her mouth with the heel of her hand.

"Okay, that was unexpected," she pants slightly, sucking in some fresh air.

"Has that happened before?" I ask, slightly worried.

She shakes her head and takes the bottle of water I'd been holding for her from my hand. After she takes a tentative sip, she looks at me. "First time, but I've been wondering if it would hit me. Doc said it can start at around six weeks."

"I'm sorry," I tell her almost helplessly and with a huge bolt of guilt that she has to go through this. "That just sucks."

"It's fine," she says with a brave smile. She reaches into her front pocket and pulls out her car keys. "But I think I'm going to run out to my car and get some gum. I wouldn't want to be talking to anyone with vomit breath today."

"Are you sure you don't want me to take you home?" I offer.

Her smile stays in place, but her eyes flash with warning. Her words are slow and deliberate. "I'm fine, Bodie. It's just some minor morning sickness. I feel better already."

I stare at her dubiously. Her face is tinged green, I think.

Not sure.

"Well, let me run out to your car for you," I say as I extend my hand for her keys. "I'll get your gum."

Rachel doesn't hand me her keys. Instead, she steps closer to me. Her voice is low, so no one can hear. "Bodie… I'm fine. I'm also perfectly able to walk to my car and back. Don't treat me like I'm fragile."

And then I understand.

Rachel is a tough cookie, for sure. I get that part. But more importantly, we are standing in front of all her coworkers, some of whom she'll be on a mission with next week. She can't show any weakness at all, in any form.

Giving her an understanding nod, I step back from her. I sweep my hand toward the patio door. "Go get your gum."

She smiles at me gratefully and moves past me. My hand flies out and slaps her on the ass and not gently, either. She yelps and tucks her butt under, shuffling quickly away from me. Looking over her shoulder, she levels a heated glare my way.

I just grin in return. "Not going to treat you fragilely,

and don't bother looking at me like that. I happen to know you like having your ass slapped."

And Jesus… fucking adorable.

Pink stains Rachel's cheeks.

She spins away and trots through the door, and I know my laugh follows her all the way.

CHAPTER 12

Rachel

HARD COPIES OF schematics of the diesel tanker are spread across the huge conference room table. There's a projected image on the screen that is suspended mechanically from the ceiling. It's got several pictures of men—all headshots—laid out in rows. It's the main crew of the tanker. Kynan stands at the screen going over their bios, arms crossed as he rocks back and forth on the balls of his feet. He's in his element, having effortlessly stepped to the helm of The Jameson Group after its founder, Jerico Jameson, retired to run The Wicked Horse full time.

Doesn't mean that Jerico is fully out of the game, though. He's sitting at the other end of the conference table, scribbling notes on a legal pad while Kynan talks. Jerico will often come into our intel and planning sessions as a consultant. He doesn't get paid to throw in his expertise and advice, but does so only because he still loves this company even if he's not running it anymore.

We leave in two days to escort the tanker through the Strait of Malacca, an incredibly important trade route between China and India. A quarter of the world's seaborne oil travels through the strait and thus makes it a very tempting target for pirates. There will be almost twenty-four hours of commercial travel to Singapore, four days on the tanker where we'll work in three-to-four men, twelve-hour shifts patrolling and guarding the ship with fifty-caliber mounted machine guns. All in all, we should be back to the States within a week if all goes well.

Which it should.

Not all merchants are willing to pay the hefty price for private security, but those who do make sure it's well known they are protected. I fully expect our ship will be left alone, but that's no guarantee.

I'm satisfied with our team and I've been on ops with all of them before at one time or another except for our newest member, Merrit Gables. He's only been with Jameson for two months, coming to us straight out of a Navy SEALs enlistment.

Cage, Sal, and Benji will be on the mission, and the last member of our team is Kara Hathaway. She's a ball-busting blonde who saw a lot of combat action in the Army as a member of a cultural support team. Her main purpose was to question Afghan women, but her job was every bit as dangerous as the special forces she attached with. She went on all raids with them and has some of the most harrowing war stories I've ever heard. She also has four black belts in different martial arts and I think she's personally hoping the tanker gets boarded so she can beat the shit out of some pirates.

"Benji will lead Team One. Bodie, Kara, and Merrit will be under him," Kynan says as he uncrosses his arms and leans over to place his palms on the table. He looks around the group and continues, "Team Two will be led by Rachel. Sal and Cage… you're with her. Team One will cover night shifts since that's the most likely time for an attack. Two has the day shift."

There's a faint rustling around the table as we know the meeting is wrapping up. Beside me, Sal raises his hand slightly to get Kynan's attention.

Kynan looks his way. "What's up?"

"I'm sure I'll be an ass for asking this," he says carefully, "but I would like some assurances that Hart is up to the task of this mission."

A flash of heat boils me from the inside out, and my head snaps to the right to glare at Sal. His eyes are pinned on Kynan, though.

"She's up to the task," I hear from across the table, and I slowly turn to look at Bodie. He has cold, hard eyes locked onto Sal, daring him to argue.

Sal looks across to Bodie and his voice is neutral, refusing to engage in a fight. "With all due respect, Wright, I'd like something more than your word since you're involved with her."

I flush even hotter that my personal sex life is now out on the table as a concern for this mission.

"Rachel has medical clearance," Kynan says in a tone that causes all heads to swivel his way. "She's got two doctors who have verified she's fine to go on any missions for the first trimester."

"Again," Sal says with determination to make his voice heard. "I'm sure she's healthy and fit, but what if something were to happen to her out on the tanker? I don't want to be a downer, but we need to consider that as a possibility. There's not going to be adequate medical care, and then we're down a team member."

To my surprise, Jerico stands up from the end of the table. He slides his hands casually into the pockets of his dress pants. "It's why we're sending a team of seven rather than six. If something happens to Rachel, Bodie moves to her team. Sal… you'd take over as leader. Rachel knows the risks and accepts them."

At this point, my emotions are all over the place. I'm pissed Sal would question my abilities, even if there's something deep inside of me that admits he's right to have the concern. I'm healthy, strong, and capable as anyone at this table. But it doesn't mean I'd stay that way.

I'm also conflicted about Bodie defending me. There's a part of me that thinks it's sweet, because he knows how important this job is to me. But there's a part that hates him doing so, too, because really… he's not a credible source given his involvement with me.

"Fair enough," Sal says, and then his voice drops two octaves. "One last thing… I'd like to respectfully disagree with the choice of Hart to lead the team. I think I'm better qualified and well… not prone to emotions."

My head snaps back his way. There's no denying Sal is the shit and could do as good a job running the team as me, but now he's questioning my true abilities despite my pregnancy.

"I can assure you that I'm able to do this job without any issues," I snarl. I don't look at Bodie across from me, but I can see out of the corner of my eye when he straightens in his chair.

Sal's not deterred by the sensitive nature of our discussion, nor how it borders on sexism and misogyny. "Hart… in the last week, I've seen you have an emotional breakdown at the gym and toss your cookies from the smell of a hamburger. I've got the right to ask these questions."

Fuck… I know he does. I know it and I hate it, and I don't know how to deal with it. Maybe I should bow out and just let him lead the team.

Maybe I should just stay behind and let someone else take my team.

"You two should battle it out," Jerico says nonchalantly. All heads swing his way.

He looks right at me. "Hart… he's got legit concerns."

I nod reluctantly.

Jerico looks to Sal. "I think she's capable but if you want her to prove it, battle it out."

"What do you suggest?" Sal asks with his jaw locked.

Jerico gives a casual shrug as if he has no formalized plan, but I can see that he does. "Three events. You each pick one, I'll pick the third. Best two out of three wins the honors of leading Team Two."

"Knives," Sal says quickly, leveling me with a satisfied smirk. Asshole picked that because he saw how badly I did and the resulting meltdown I had.

"Shooting," I say, taking great satisfaction in watching him swallow hard. Sal is a good shot. One of the best at Jameson. I'm a million times better, though.

"And the third event?" I ask Jerico as I turn to look back up at him.

He shoots a look at Kynan, who gives a shrug. Jerico taps his chin as if deep in thought, but then he finally announces with a big grin. "A hot-dog eating contest."

"A what?" I ask in bewilderment.

Sal gives a low, dark laugh that is totally gleeful in an evil way. I'm sure he's banking on me hurling my guts up from the smell.

Yeah, well fuck you, Sal. There's no way in hell I'm losing this competition.

I turn to look back at Jerico. "Deal. Let's get started."

Everyone starts chattering, and I vaguely hear a few people laying down bets. I glance across the table at

Bodie, and he's staring at me. At first, I can't read a damn thing on his face, but I've spent a lot of time staring at it this past week. I've become adept at reading the nuances.

It starts to become clear to me. He's frustrated my abilities are being questioned, and he's a little worried about something happening to me while out on the boat with no medical help. He's also burning with a need for me to avenge myself, all while being put out that he can't do it for me.

It's a lot of fucking emotion brewing in him, but all I can do is give him a confident smile. His in return is tight and guarded.

I want to tell him "I got this," but I'm not sure he'd believe me.

♦

"YOU OKAY?" BODIE asks with a quick glance as he pulls my Maserati into my driveway. He asks because the motion of the car is making me nauseous, which is in turn making me sweat and pant.

"I'm fine," I say through gritted teeth as he brings the car to a halt. As soon as he puts it in park, I've got the passenger door open and I'm puking my guts up all over my driveway.

Ten hot dogs and buns.

Which means I throw up for quite a long time.

I'm vaguely aware of Bodie standing just outside of

the range of vomit, patiently waiting for me to get it all out.

When I'm done, my head swims and I sit back in the car seat, breathing hard. My head rolls on the headrest, and I look at him balefully.

He grins back. "You were fucking awesome."

My smile is weak but genuine. "I was, wasn't I?"

As expected, Sal creamed me in the knife throwing and I wiped the floor with him on the shooting range. When Jerico had twenty hot dogs brought in from Pink's and laid ten each out on opposite sides of the conference room table, my stomach started churning.

Sal sat across from me, cracking his knuckles and already smiling in victory as he took in the pale green tint of my skin and the sweat beaded on my brow. Morning sickness really sucked ass. It hasn't been plaguing me too bad, and is easily controlled by nibbling on a few crackers, but ten greasy hot dogs?

It may have been the hardest thing I've ever done in my life.

The competition was simple. Whoever could eat ten hot dogs in the fastest time was the winner. That meant fully swallowed, nothing left behind. There was also a five-minute puke clause added, where the hot dogs had to stay down that length of time to be declared the victor.

Despite the nausea and violent need to hurl, I cleared my mind and swallowed hot dog after hot dog. All I could think about was taking Bodie's cock down my throat, and that had to have helped in some way. Sal still had half a hot dog left when I swallowed my last bite.

It was agony waiting out that five minutes, and even when it was up and I was declared the winner and resounding leader of Team Two—Sal gave me a grudging handshake after—I still refused to puke.

I did not, however, hesitate to ask Bodie to drive me home. I had some serious shakes by the time we got in my car, and I moaned and groaned all the way home.

Right now, I'm feeling a little bit better. The fact Bodie thought what I did was awesome makes it an even better victory.

"Thank you," I tell him softly, looking at him across my pile of vomit. "For defending me in there. Supporting me."

"It's nothing," he says nonchalantly.

"For trusting me to do my job," I add. That's really what I'm grateful for. "For not holding me back, even though I know damn well you're worried about me going."

Bodie doesn't respond other than to wave his hand. "Come on. Let's get you out of the car and inside. Maybe some ginger ale for you."

With a sigh, I swing my legs out and deftly sidestep the vomit. I'll come out later and rinse it off. When I meet him, I tug gently on the bottom of his t-shirt to get his attention. "No. Seriously. Thank you for not fighting me on going on this mission. For letting me do this. I know you could raise a stink about it, so I know you're taking a risk right along with me."

"Doctor said you were cleared, right?" he asks, although he knows this is so. Dr. Anchors wrote a letter to Dr. McCullough, and it's in my employment file.

I nod. "And I feel fantastic. Except for a little nausea. As long as I stash some saltines in my duffel when we leave, it will be fine."

"Then there's no need to worry," he says lightly.

None, I think to myself. *Other than the fact I've had a miscarriage before.*

Dr. Anchors spent a lot of time telling me that meant nothing. He said most miscarriages are a one-time thing, and the majority of women go on to have healthy pregnancies after.

I feel guilty because I've made a conscious decision not to tell Bodie about my miscarriage. I didn't feel it relevant after talking privately to Dr. Anchors, and I did it for a very selfish reason. I knew that Bodie would have increased worry if he knew. He might even fight me on going out on missions.

So, I chose to keep that to myself and hope and pray for the best that this baby will continue to stay healthy and the pregnancy will be normal. There's going to be a time soon where I won't be able to go out on missions, so I want to take every opportunity to do so.

I hope that doesn't make me a bad person, but I still have to preserve some part of myself because when this is all said and done, I'm going to lose a big part of me.

CHAPTER 13

Bodie

THERE'S A SLIGHT crackle of static in my earpiece before Benji's voice comes across. "We have a potential hostile bearing 325 at four nautical miles on course 180 at fifty knots. I want the team on the port side."

"Shit," I mutter, but then state louder into the thin wire microphone that runs from my earpiece, along the bottom of my cheekbone and ends just before the corner of my mouth, "Roger that."

The fact Benji has us moving to one side of the ship tells me that whatever they see on radar is of a size that worries them.

Not a big boat.

A smaller vessel that's traveling at a high rate of speed toward us.

If these are pirates, they are in for a huge surprise when they get in range. The Thai shipping company that hired us for security has wised up after two of their tankers have been robbed in the last seven months. They've equipped their ships with expensive radars and badass security professionals with very big guns.

This type of piracy is very sophisticated and has become a major criminal enterprise in Asia. Vessels like the one we're on with a low freeboard—the distance that separates the surface of the water from the top deck—makes it easy for a band of pirates to stealthily board an unsuspecting ship. Once the crew is overpowered and communications disabled, a larger boat is brought in to siphon off the black gold.

Bad news for the pirates. This tanker isn't so unsuspecting anymore.

I make it to the port side, noting Kara is already stationed at one of two Browning fifty caliber machine guns we have temporarily mounted on each side of the ship. She nods at me while double checking the ammunition belt, which is equipped with tracers so the pirates can see the bullets coming in the dark of the night.

My adrenaline spikes, and a pleasantly antsy feeling makes my heart beat a little faster. These are the situations I love best when I'm working with The Jameson Group.

I turn away from Kara and head toward the bow, where another gun is mounted. Merrit will be on that one. I'll patrol in between with my night-vision goggles, reporting to Benji who is in the control room with the captain.

A door to my left bursts open, startling me for a moment before I realize it's Rachel. She's got her M27 automatic rifle strapped over her shoulder and a pistol holstered at her hip. She looks bright eyed, even though I know she was sleeping soundly not fifteen minutes ago when I did a quick check on her. She's on day shift and I'm on night, so we've not seen each other much the last two days.

"What are you doing up here?" I ask.

"I heard Benji on the comms. Figured I'd come lend a hand. Sal and Cage are coming up, too."

"We've got it covered," I tell her curtly.

Her chin jerks inward, and she blinks at me in surprise. "You got it covered? Since when does any teammate refuse another's help?"

"Since we have two Browning's that we'll unload on them before they can get anywhere close to this ship," I tell her confidently. "Once they realize we're armed, they're going to turn tail and run."

Rachel narrows her eyes somewhat. "If that's the case," she says slowly as she removes her rifle from her back and sets it against the wall. "No sense in me lugging this around. But I think I'll just stay and watch for funsies."

"Rachel," I say in exasperation. "Go back to bed. Get some rest. You have a shift starting in about four hours."

"Not tired," she says stubbornly. "I'll just hang with you guys and watch the action. The tracers are pretty at night."

Frustration hits me hard, followed by an anxious squeezing to my chest. "I don't want you up here—"

Rachel's eyes flash with fury. "*You* don't want *me* up here?"

I refuse to answer, setting my jaw into a stubborn clamp of tightness.

"What is it, Bodie?" she asks sarcastically. "Getting on the bandwagon with your other buddies who think I'm inferior now that I'm pregnant? Think my emotions might overwhelm me? Make me a danger to you?"

"That's not what I'm—"

She rolls right over me. "Or maybe it's just that I'm a woman? Not quite as strong as you. Is that it?"

"No, Rachel," I say angrily. My blood boils that she would even think that.

"Oh, I know," she says, getting in my face. "It's because I'm your brood mare, isn't it? Got your baby inside of me, and you want that precious cargo tucked—"

My hands shoot to the sides of her head, and I take in her wide eyes and the little "o" her mouth forms into. I press my thumbs under her jaw to close her mouth, and yank her to me so my face is hovering right over hers. "I don't want anything to happen to *you*. It's got nothing to do with your abilities or the pregnancy. It's about *you*, you dumbass."

She blinks at me in confusion.

Again, she blinks.

She stays silent. Thank fuck for that.

"I would worry about *you*," I continue in a gentler tone. "And that would make me ineffective."

"But there's no danger," she says in a raspy voice, her jaw working against the pressure of my thumbs. I release my hold on her and take a step back.

"If they have guns like ours," I say in a defeated voice. "Then there's great danger."

"I'm more than capable—"

"It only takes one stray bullet," I cut her off. With a sigh I lean over and pick her gun back up. I push it at her, and she takes it almost reluctantly. "But I also know that it's wrong of me to ask you to go hide just to appease me. This is what you do, Rachel."

Her eyes hold mine, and I wonder if she's actually going to appease me and go below. The moment is broken when Benji comes across our comms. "Suspected hostile a mile out, course unchanged. Take positions."

There's no time to debate this further with Rachel. Cage and Sal come out of the same door that Rachel had just a few moments ago. She orders them to position as backup to Kara and Merrit on the port guns.

Before she turns to leave, she reaches a hand out and touches the back of mine briefly.

"Stay safe," she murmurs.

"You too."

Then she's gone.

The blaring of the ship's horns—two long blows—is

the indication to the crew that danger is approaching, and they are to get below deck. There's a scrambling around of the few night-shift members, but it doesn't take a lot to run a small tanker like this. There are only twelve crew members, and they'll all be below to minimize injuries. The exception is the captain and navigator, who will stay in the control room with Benji. If pirates were somehow to make it past us, there's a fifth Browning in there set up on a tripod aimed at the door. No one is getting in without Benji's say-so.

I see the light of the speeding boat just before Benji announces, "Two thousand yards out. Merrit and Kara… at your will."

The approaching boat is closer to the stern, which is Merrit's gun. It's coming at a high rate of speed with no signs of slowing, so it's clear their intentions are nefarious. As such, Merrit doesn't wait. He lets loose, the booming noise of the machine gun drowning out everything. Tracers light up the bullets' trajectories, helping Merrit to keep his aim just short of the approaching boat. At the same time, Kara lets loose a volley of bullets, spraying the water from bow to midship, letting the approaching pirates know we're heavily armed.

I stand braced, my own M27 trained on the boat. I want to look to my right, lay my eyes just briefly on Rachel to know exactly where she's positioned, but I can't.

The ear-splitting bursts of rounds lasts no more than ten seconds in totality, but it's enough that the approaching speedboat now five hundred yards out swings hard to the right, throwing a wave of seafoam outward at the abrupt maneuver. For a moment, I think the boat might tip over. It's close enough to the lighting of the tanker that I can make out perhaps ten men on board, some with rifles. They grab hard onto railings so as not to pitch over the side, and while I can't quite make out the detail, I suspect their faces are masks of fury and frustration they won't be sacking this vessel.

Within moments, the boat is out of sight and soon out of earshot. Benji will be watching it carefully on radar, but I seriously doubt they'll be coming back. If they had weaponry to rival ours, we'd have seen it. Besides, they have to know we have radar capabilities by how quick we were to defend our space.

Yeah... pretty sure these pirates are just shit of out luck when it comes to this tanker. I expect the added benefit to tonight's attempted raid is that word will pass that this shipping company has put the money into security and won't be trifled with. The pirates will move on to a weaker prey, but I'm betting more and more companies will be hiring companies like Jameson to escort them through dangerous waters.

"Hold positions," Benji instructs over the comms, but that was unnecessary chatter. It's protocol to do so after an aborted attack, just in case they make a quick turnaround for a foolish second run.

To my surprise, Rachel slings her rifle over her shoulder and comes walking my way. She's technically not on duty. Had Benji needed her, Cage, and Sal, he would have called them up.

I hold my place against the railing at midship although I harness my rifle as well.

"That was exciting," Rachel says drolly when she reaches me. She leans her hip against the rail, resting her arm on the top. The swishing sound of sea spray as the tanker cuts through the water is almost relaxing in a way, particularly now the adrenaline has waned.

"For Merrit and Kara at least," I reply. "They got to fire the big guns."

She doesn't respond, but looks out over the black water. I turn my head that way as well.

"I don't think we should go on ops together," I tell her carefully.

Rachel shrugs. "It's not like I have many more to go on. I'm sure Kynan will cut me out after the first trimester is up. He won't have any problem assigning us to different teams."

"Just the really dangerous stuff," I clarify. Because fuck if I can concentrate on what I'm doing if I'm worried about her. I hated admitting that to her, but she sort of forced it from me.

"I understand," she replies quietly, still looking out over the water. "But concert security isn't so dangerous, right?"

Chuckling, I turn to look at her. The breeze is whipping the shorter locks of her hair that have fallen out of her little ponytail. "No, I wouldn't worry about you quite the same providing concert security versus going up against pirates."

"I'm sorry you worry about me," Rachel says, taking a step in closer to me. "I wish you wouldn't."

I don't even need special skills at reading between the lines here, because her meaning is blatantly clear.

What I'm sure she really means is, *I'm sorry you worry about me because I just don't really feel the same about you.*

While Rachel has warmed up to me tremendously over the last three weeks, I still know that this will never be anything more than what it is right now. We're sharing an experience—childbirth—and because we're wildly attracted to each other, we're using the baby as an excuse to continue fucking each other. I know damn well had Rachel not gotten pregnant, we would have never hooked up again. We barely spoke to each other unless it was work related in those weeks in between the first time we were together and when she found out she was pregnant.

I don't respond to her last statement. No need to. I'm not going to stop worrying, and she's not going to stop wanting me not to worry. Instead, I nod back toward the door that leads below deck. "You should go get some sleep. Your shift will be here before you know it."

As if the mere suggestion of sleep hits her body in a physical way, she gives a long yawn followed by a sheepish grin. "Yeah... I could use a little more sleep. Call me if the pirates come back."

I laugh and shake my head. "You know *that* I will not do. I hope you sleep through any potential attack that may come."

Rachel then does something so uncharacteristic I almost doubt I'm seeing it. She wrinkles up her nose and sticks her tongue out at me like a petulant five-year-old. It's fucking adorable, but before I can even laugh, she's spins around and heads for the door.

I take a few moments to admire her ass as she walks away from me. It's a great ass... round and toned. I wonder how her body is going to be changing over the next few weeks. It won't be long before that flat tummy gets a little bump going, and the thought of it turns me on.

What a fucking perv I've turned into, but I can't be too abashed. Everything about Rachel Hart turns me on, and it did long before I ever fucked her. I've always had the hots for her like every other dude at Jameson. I'm just the lucky bastard who is currently fucking her, and fucking her exclusively.

It will totally suck when it's over.

And it would be over. There is simply no way I can make it work—being a single father and leading this type of career. In fact, as soon as we make it past the twelve-week mark, I plan to tell my parents about what's going on. They'll need to get ready for their oldest son to move back home. The farmhouse is big and sprawling, but even I know it's going to be a tight fit with the baby and me in there along with everyone else.

We'll make it work, though. The Wrights always have. And I know there's no way in hell my mom will have it any other way. She's not going to let me or her grandbaby out of her sight for a while, but I'm sure I'll get my own place one day. Maybe build something small on my parents' land.

It would be hard readjusting to farm life. I'm not averse to the hard work at all, but I am opposed to a mundane life, and that is what will await me in the Nebraska cornfields.

Oh, well. It's a sacrifice that will be totally worth it once that baby comes.

That I know without a doubt.

CHAPTER 14

Rachel

I STRUT THROUGH the Social Room of the Wicked Horse, having just stepped out of the lobby elevator. I'm wearing my sexiest dress—a low-cut number in silvery ice blue that compliments my eyes. It barely covers my ass, and any slight bending forward will reveal I'm not wearing panties.

Normally when I come off a high-speed, dangerous op, I'm totally amped to work out the excess energy at The Wicked Horse.

Add in the fact that I'm having the best sex of my life with Bodie, and I've got raging hormones coursing through me, I can barely contain myself right now. I need Bodie, and I need him bad. There's a little bit of shame in the fact that he knew it, too, because as we were landing at McCarran in a private jet yesterday, he leaned over and whispered in my ear, "Tomorrow night. You and I are going to tear up the club."

Bodie texted me a bit ago, and said he was coming

out a little earlier than we had planned. He wanted to play some poker with the other team members in The Apartment for a bit.

As I walk past the long bar that takes up one wall of the room, I notice Jerico standing at the end. I hardly ever see him here anymore and never without Trista. He waves a hand at me and nods down at the drink he's got sitting before him, a silent invitation to come join him. I'd rather get to Bodie, but there's something to be said for building up the anticipation.

By the time I make it to Jerico, he has a ginger ale over ice waiting for me. I would have preferred water since I'm not nauseous, but the sentiment is nice, so I don't say anything.

"All caught up on your sleep and the time difference?" he asks. It's a standard question after traveling halfway around the world but over the years, I've trained myself to sleep on the flights to help with my bounce back.

"I'm good to go," I tell him as I take a sip of the ginger ale, leaning my forearm on the bar.

"Sounds like you guys had a bit of excitement out there," he says conversationally. I'm sure Kynan told him all about what happened with the pirates coming at us and turning tail when we fired warning shots their way from the Browning. There's a slight twinkle in Jerico's eye, and I know he misses this life on occasion.

"Where's Trista?" I ask as I look around.

Jerico picks up his whiskey from the bar, takes a sip, and replies, "On her way here. Where's Bodie?"

I grin. Clearly Kynan's been filling him in on more than just how the operation went. "Kynan's been blabbing, huh?"

"I admit I heard about the infamous pregnancy announcement you made at Kynan's party a couple of weeks ago and how you also kissed him after. But even if I hadn't known that, I would have figured it out during the competition you had with Sal. Bodie paced all around with worry during each contest. It was written all over his face."

"Ironic he's in The Apartment right now playing poker," I say with a small smile, swishing my ginger ale around in my glass. I take another small sip. "He sort of wears his heart on his sleeve."

"Sounds like that bothers you," Jerico observes thoughtfully.

I've known Jerico a long time. Over ten years since I came to work at Jameson, the company he founded. We're friends, but not overly tight. Still, he's perceptive and doesn't have any stake in Jameson anymore. He could be a sounding board for me, because I'm finding myself having mixed feelings on practically everything.

"When the pirates were approaching, Bodie didn't want me up there. Said he would worry about me too much, and it would make him ineffective," I tell Jerico.

Jerico shrugs. "So?"

"So, I'm pregnant with his baby, currently fucking him exclusively, and he's developing feelings for me. This spells disaster."

"Have you two agreed this was just casual?" he asks with concern on his face.

"We have," I say with a nod. "But can it really be casual when there's a baby involved?"

Jerico takes another sip of his drink. When he sets it down, he leans in toward me. "Okay, no bullshitting me, Rachel... everyone knows you're pregnant and it's Bodie's, but I haven't heard what the game plan is. Are y'all going to raise the baby together?"

Clearly, Kynan has kept some things secret.

I give a shake of my head, and the fact I can't look at him when I do that seems to suggest to me that I must have some shame in my decision.

"So, what are you two going to do?" he asks curiously. There's no condemnation in his tone, so I look back to him.

"I um... I'm just not ready to be a mom at this stage in my life," I tell him softly. "Bodie though... he wants the baby. I agreed to carry it for him, and well... I think he's going to go back home to Nebraska, so his parents can help. Clearly, he couldn't stay here and do this type of work as a single dad."

"It would be tough," Jerico concurs, his gaze traveling slowly down my front to land on my belly. I lower my face so I can see what has his attention, and I'm stunned to see my hand resting on my stomach, rubbing in gentle, wide circles.

A loving caress right over where my abdomen will soon start extending. I'm already feeling like my pants are a bit tight on me, so I kind of expect any day now to wake up with a baby bump.

My hand falls away. I'm startled by the realization I was doing that subconsciously. I look up to Jerico guiltily, and I see it written all over his face.

Your brain might be saying you're not ready to be a mom, but your heart may have some different ideas.

Fuck.

Just fuck.

No.

Fuck, I can't even think like that.

I set the ginger ale I'd been holding with my other hand down and give him a tight smile. "Well, I better go find Bodie. I'm sure he's wondering where I am."

"Of course," Jerico says with a gallant nod of his head. "Enjoy yourself tonight."

"Oh, I intend to," I reply a little too rambunctiously, and Jerico snorts.

I turn away from him, tingles already settling in between my legs at the prospect of being with Bodie soon. I stop, though, when Jerico calls out my name.

Looking over my shoulder at him, I raise an eyebrow.

"If you want to talk it through and need an impartial sounding board, I've got your back. No judgments here."

This time, my smile is generous and grateful. "Thanks, Jerico. That means a lot."

Because one of the things that has been giving me trouble lately is how others are going to view me when it comes to light that I'm giving the baby to Bodie. I'm going to be vilified, I know. How could a woman—a mother—give her child up when she's perfectly capable of raising it herself?

At least, that's the question I keep asking myself several times a day. How can I do this?

How will I be able to live with myself after? Will the regrets destroy me? Will my actions destroy my child?

My head swims with the damage that could be done by one decision I've made.

I give a mental shake, forcing those thoughts away. They have no place in The Wicked Horse. This club is about forgetting reality for a bit and immersing in fantasy.

That is what I'm going to do with the one man who is rocking my world so hard I'm not sure I even recognize it anymore.

I get my swagger back, strutting from The Social Room to the hub just outside the doors. From there, I can take a number of hallways leading to the different-themed rooms, but I choose the one that goes back to The Apartment.

The private club within a private club and where currently several members of the Jameson Group are all hanging out.

Bodie's eyes come to me the minute I walk through the door, the bouncer standing there giving me a nod of recognition when I pass by his bulky form. My eyes stay on Bodie while I wind my way through some of the patrons standing around chatting. I sidestep a couple wildly kissing while the woman jacks the man off without a care in the world.

That's what I want tonight.

Not a care in the world except for Bodie and feeling amazing pleasure at each other's hands.

As I get closer, I go ahead and spare a glance at the other players. I bristle just slightly when I see Sal sitting there. Our relationship has been somewhat strained since I beat him at the hot-dog-eating contest, although I suspect it has something more to do with some underlying misogyny on his part. I also see Cage, Kara, and Merrit sitting there. The only one missing is Benji, but he doesn't hang out here too much.

The poker table seats eight, and it's filled. I don't recognize the other three men who are playing, although one of them is making fuck-me eyes at Kara as she sits opposite him. She's definitely getting laid tonight.

So am I for that matter.

Kara looks up to see me approaching from where she sits next to Bodie. Her face lights up, and she says, "About damn time you got here."

I move around the table and come to stand beside

Bodie's chair. He pushes it back slightly and his arm comes around the back of my legs, pulling me in a little closer so I'm leaning on the side of his seat. I can see his poker hand, and it sucks. I watch as the betting goes around the table.

I'm not really paying attention, though. I'm having a tough time with it when Bodie's hand spreads wide on my outer thigh, and he strokes lightly up and down. I rest my hand on his shoulder, leaning into him a bit further.

His hand moves to the back of my thigh before slipping in between. I go still as his hand moves higher. Bodie sucks in his breath slightly when he realizes I'm not wearing panties, and I get dizzy when his fingers prod at my slick entrance.

Lightly grazing his fingers through my swollen lips, he studies his cards and jokes with the other players as the betting goes higher with each person. How in the hell he can carry on conversation is beyond me, because I can barely even think straight.

I lean into him a little more, scooting my leg out to give him more access.

He doesn't take it, though, making me crazy by the lazy movements of his fingers giving me no penetration or touch to my clit where I really need it.

When the betting gets to Kara, who is seated on the other side of Bodie, I'm startled when Bodie pushes a finger slowly into me. Had he gone fast and deep, I would have cried out and probably orgasmed, but as it is, he has me vibrating with the need for something more and I can barely breathe.

Kara places her bet, and all eyes turn to Bodie.

Perhaps to the casual observer, he just looks like a guy with his hand on perhaps his girl's ass. Only I know that it's deep between my legs with a single digit flexing gently inside me.

Bodie pretends to study his cards in contemplation for a moment, and I say pretend because he has nothing worth anything. He needs to fold.

But he doesn't right away because he's putting on a show for me. Slowly, he pulls the finger out and pushes it back in. I'm in danger of passing out because my lungs aren't working. He pulls it out again, and then with flourish, he tosses his cards face down and says, "I'm out."

He pushes two fingers back inside, all the way to the third knuckle, and it's not gentle at all. I gasp, and finally my lungs are working. I suck air back in, not able to help the way my hips tilt to try to draw him in deeper.

Bodie likes my visible reaction. To my consternation, as well as my delight, he starts to finger fuck me right there at the table. I'm vaguely aware of the betting moving to the person on Bodie's left, but mostly I'm aware I've got no control over my body.

With Bodie's fingers pumping in and out of me, I can't stop the circling of my hips or the tiny moans slithering up my throat and out of my mouth. Bodie's free hand drops down to his lap, and he palms his erection through his jeans. I lift my face, lock my gaze on Merrit sitting across from me, and I flush with embarrassment when I realize he's fully engaged in watching this spectacle.

My eyes go around the table, and I see that everyone's watching.

"Oh, God," I mutter. Yet, I don't want it to stop. My hand clutches Bodie's shoulder, gripping a hunk of his t-shirt tightly to hang on.

"I can't fucking concentrate," Cage says with a dark laugh, and my gaze snaps to his. He's staring right between my legs, which are now spread—when did that happen?—and I realize he can clearly see what Bodie's doing to me.

I'm torn between the need to come while all of these people watch Bodie destroy my resistance, and the need to run out of here in embarrassment because I'm letting him do it to me.

The decision is taken out of my hands when Bodie abruptly removes his hand and rises from his chair. He takes me by the hand and pulls me roughly around the table, walking swiftly toward the exit door.

"Get it, Bodie," someone calls out from the table behind us. Sal maybe?

I have no clue where he's taking me, but wherever it is, I hope it's not far. We leave The Apartment, walk to the end of the hall, and then hang a left followed by an immediate right down the hall to The Silo.

My favorite room.

We don't even make it to the interior once we enter, instead cutting down the back perimeter hall that leads to the entrances to the glassed-in room.

He pushes open the first door we come to, and I'm surprised to see a couple rolling on a silk-covered mattress. They're partially dressed, so they must have just gotten started. There are a few people sitting on a couch in front of the glass wall looking in, idly sipping wine and talking while the action unfolds.

The couple raise their heads... a man and a woman who look to be in their mid-thirties. They smile at us in invitation, but Bodie shuts that shit down quickly.

"I'll give you a thousand bucks each if you vacate this room immediately," he growls.

Neither hesitate, rolling right off the mattress and gathering their discarded shirts.

Bodie reaches into his back pocket, and pulls his wallet out. He pulls a credit card out and hands it to the guy. "Go have some drinks at the bar on me. I'll find you in a bit and make arrangements to get you paid."

"You got it," the guy says with a grin as he grabs the card in one hand and his woman in the other.

In moments, we're left alone in the room.

I watch as Bodie walks confidently over to the glass wall. With a tug on a silk rope with a tassel, he closes the heavy gray curtains so no one can see in.

"Want privacy now, huh?" I ask as he turns to look at me.

"Gave enough of a show already," he says as he walks back to me.

Stalks me rather.

I feel hunted, and it turns me on.

I'm not sure how it happens, but Bodie and I land on the mattress. His mouth is on me, his hands pulling at my clothes. Rolling around, we kiss, grope, and get naked. His hand goes back between my legs, and he hums low in his throat when he finds me just as wet for him.

He flips me on my back, spreading my legs by pushing his in between. Fisting his hard cock in one hand, he presses it to my pussy and starts to fill me up. I raise my legs, spreading myself further, and my hands go to his chest for leverage. I tilt my hips to suck him in, and in a fluidly beautiful move, he's got his pelvis pressed to mine.

Bodie then does something so sweetly intimate. He lays his body fully on mine, pressing his weight down onto me. His hands come to mine, fingers intertwining, and he raises my arms above my head.

I get a soft kiss from him, then he nuzzles my neck as he starts to move slowly inside of me. My hands grip his tight as I lock my ankles at his lower back. His back hunches slightly so he can get a better angle, and then he's driving into me with slow strokes that go impossibly deep. After he plunges to the hilt, he grinds against me and my clit becomes absolutely engorged.

It takes no time at all before I'm hovering on the brink in pure ecstasy. Bodie's movements never get faster, but instead become more deliberate. A slow fucking meant to consume us both. His breath is hot against my neck as he whispers, "Want you to come for me, Rachel."

My name crosses his lips as he punches his hips deep, and I splinter apart with a hoarse cry of abandonment. Bodie groans in appreciation, goes still inside of me, and then lifts his head up to stare at me while he orgasms.

The veins stick out in his temples, and the muscles in his throat go tight as he shudders in my arms. He keeps his eyes locked onto me the entire time he releases in me, and I don't know that I've ever felt closer to a human being in my life.

When he's empty, Bodie drops his forehead to mine. "Fuck, that was good."

"The best," I murmur in reply as my fingers play gently with the hair at the nape of his neck.

"Was that awkward in The Apartment?" he asks, lifting so I can look into his eyes again.

"You mean you finger fucking me in front of our coworkers?" I ask with a grin. "Yeah… a little. I mean, no one in Jameson has ever fucked around before and in such a public manner."

"Yet, we've all watched each other fuck here in the club," he points out.

"I know. And there was a small part of me that was totally turned on by it."

"Me too." He chuckles and then presses another kiss onto my mouth. "Interested in going another round in here?"

"In this room?" I ask for clarification.

"No," he says with a wicked gleam in his eye. "The room with the stocks. I'd like to lock you up in it, and let you suck my dick a little. You give the best head, Hart."

I laugh and lift my head to give him a quick kiss in return. "Deal."

"Actually, I really want to fuck you while you're locked in the stocks," he says with an almost menacing smile that causes my belly to flutter in anticipation. "Best way to spank your ass hard, which I know you happen to like."

I groan at the same time I push him off me. He's right. I like that a lot, and I'd like to go do that like right now.

Bodie laughs at my impatience as we roll off the mattress and gather our clothes. We don't bother putting them on as we're just going down two rooms.

It's turning out to be a perfect night here at The Wicked Horse.

CHAPTER 15

Bodie

I TURN MY truck off as soon as I pull into Rachel's driveway, and just stare at her house for a moment while the engine continues to tick. She invited me over to dinner tonight, and I don't know what to make of it.

It's perplexing because for the last three nights, we've only been together at The Wicked Horse. Neither of us have any jobs planned this week, and I never saw her in the gym when I was there working out. But like clockwork, I'd get a text from her late afternoon that invited me to meet her at The Wicked Horse.

One thought is that now that we've come out in the open, she likes the thrill of us having sex in front of others. It's sort of taboo or forbidden, and not going to lie, I get a rush from the guys at Jameson watching me with her. But I also like my alone time with her as well.

The other thought is that Rachel is using the club as a barrier between us. It's impersonal and casual, or at least on the face of things. But what I do to her and with her is anything but, and she damn well knows it.

Why she is now inviting me into her home for dinner is troubling. I'm more apt to believe she's going to lay something dreadful on me, like she's changed her mind about carrying the baby.

With a sigh because I'll never know until I just walk in there, I hop out of the truck and head up to her house. When I knock on the door, she calls from the inside, "It's open."

I walk into Rachel's living room, barely noticing the ergonomic lines of her contemporary furniture or that her decor lends a spartan feel. Minimalist artwork and no personal photos anywhere. Not that I have any except a few of my family in my bedroom, but I'm a dude. I'm not supposed to be into that shit.

Upon first inhale once I cross the threshold, my mouth waters. Garlic and cheese and pungent tomatoes.

Her kitchen is open to the living area, and Rachel is standing behind a long, rectangular island that separates the two rooms, cutting up a loaf of Italian bread. She smiles at me.

It's open and genuine, and I'm immediately put at ease.

"Smells delicious," I say as I take a seat on one of the bar stools on the living room side.

"Lasagna," she says as she saws through the crusty bread with a serrated knife. "Not a drop of Italian blood in me but for some reason, I make a really good lasagna.

Plus, I'm craving all kinds of gooey cheese."

"Anything I can do to help?" I ask, hoping there's not so I can just sit here and watch her be domestic. Domesticity is not something I think about when I think of Rachel Hart, so I'm going to enjoy it.

"No," she says, but then nods her head over her shoulder. "But there's a bottle of red wine on the back counter if you want some."

"I'm good." In all actuality, I love wine, but I've just not been drinking lately. Not sure if I'm just abstaining because Rachel can't drink, or if I just don't want my senses dulled when I'm around her.

Rachel nods with a small smile and finishes the bread. She lays the slices on a pan, and then dabs them with a melted butter that has garlic pieces floating in it.

"So... this is nice." She looks up at me in question, and I nod toward the bread. "You cooking dinner and inviting me."

She gives a casual shrug. "Well, like I said... I had a craving. Why not share a meal with you?"

Hmm. That's not exactly what I'd hoped to hear.

"It's occurred to me," she says casually as she pulls out the lasagna from the oven and pops in the bread. "That I don't know much about you before you came to Jameson."

I blink in surprise, taking my hungry gaze off the bubbling, cheesy casserole. Rachel is actually making conversation with me that doesn't revolve around work, sex, or the baby.

"Let's see," I say as I lean forward and prop my forearms on the counter. She mimics me and does the same from the opposite side. I try not to get distracted by her cleavage. "I knew I didn't want to work on my family's farm in Nebraska, and the military seemed like a good option. I joined the Navy right out of high school and eventually became a SEAL."

Rachel laughs and shakes her head. "You're so casual about it. But nothing about being a SEAL is casual."

I chuckle in response, because she's right about that. "Then let's just say that I might have a taste for adventure like you do."

"Why didn't you stay in the military?" she asks.

"It just wasn't for me. The rules and structure. Don't get me wrong... my time served was an amazing experience, but I didn't want it to be a long-term career."

"How did you get hired at Jameson?"

"Just some mutual contacts with Jerico, and they put me in touch with him." I lean forward with a secretive smile. "Here's a little-known fact about me. The CIA actually reached out to me, but I didn't want to be a spook. No glory in that."

Rachel laughs again, and I love the sound of it. She's always so serious, and it's nice to see her loose and relaxed. "No. Definitely no glory in that type of work."

"Jameson was definitely the right move for me. The adventure is even better, there's plenty of downtime to do my own thing, and the pay can't be beaten to be honest."

"I hear that," she says in agreement, but then her expression sobers slightly. "But seriously... you have no qualms about giving up this career to move back to Nebraska with the baby?"

"Of course, I have qualms," I say softly. "I love this job. But you can't stack up a job against family. There isn't one of my family members I wouldn't give this career up for, even down to my little second cousins who I barely see. So, you damn well better believe it will be no sacrifice to give it up for my kid."

Rachel's face crumbles slightly, and she looks down at the counter. "I must seem incredibly selfish to you then."

"God, Rachel," I exclaim, completely startled by that. Her head pops up to look at me. "I don't think you're selfish at all. You're going for what you want in life, and there's nothing wrong with that. The selfish thing would have been to get an abortion. What you're doing is the most selfless thing I've ever seen anyone do."

The timer she'd set for the bread goes off, and she looks relieved to have something else to do other than discuss this further. I watch her quietly as she pulls the bread out and sets it on top of the stove burners.

She then pulls a large knife from a drawer and proceeds to cut through the lasagna. Her back stays turned to me, her spine held stiff and straight. I want to go to her, step right into her lush backside and put my arms around her stomach. I want to press into her and assure her I don't think badly about her at all. Would my preference be she raise the child with me?

Of course. But I can't fault her for wanting a different life than me.

"Want to pull a couple of bottles of water out of the fridge for us?" she says over her shoulder as she plates up the lasagna and throws a piece of bread on each plate.

"Sure." I stand from the stool, then pull the last two bottles of water in there out, depositing them on top of the counter. "Those were your last two. Where are the others? I'll restock really quick."

Rachel nods to her left. "In the pantry there."

I open the pantry door, my eyes immediately dropping to a case of bottled water on the floor. I squat down, reach inside the plastic that had already been torn open, and start pulling out bottles. As I do, I glance at the lowest shelf and see an open box from Amazon sitting there. I lean forward, surprised at what I see.

DVD movies—*The Lion King, Frozen,* and *The Little Mermaid.* Under that are some books, and without hesitation, I lift the DVDs to see them more clearly.

Peter Rabbit.

Where the Wild Things Are.

The Giving Tree.

I glance back and forth between the box and the water bottles I continue grabbing. I suppose the argument could be made that perhaps Rachel has a niece or nephew those are for, but my gut tells me differently.

She's buying stuff for the baby.

Never for a moment do I consider that she wants to stay involved. Instead, a wave of sadness hits me that it's only about leaving a little piece of herself with the child. Nothing Rachel has done or said would lead me to believe otherwise.

♦

RACHEL COLLAPSES ON top of me, her body slick with sweat. She just rode my cock like she was riding a rodeo bull. Completely in command of the situation, pleasuring me and torturing me at the same time. She squeezed her breasts while she did so, pinching her nipples. I totally lost my shit when she started rubbing her clit while she bounced up and down on me, intent on getting herself off while doing the same for me.

I saw stars when I exploded, bucked my hips up so hard she almost fell off, and then she landed on top of me while laughing in that sexy, husky tone that said she knew she just rocked my world.

"I feel at this point I should ask what you want," I say, stroking her lower back with my hand.

Her head pops up and her eyes look at me in confusion. "What I want?"

"Yeah," I say with a sly grin. "You cook me a fabulous meal and then fuck me like I've never been fucked before. This is when the dude says, 'What do you want?'."

Rachel laughs and shakes her head. She rolls off and flips to her back beside me. "I don't want anything. I got just as much out of this as you did. Fantastic lasagna and a nuclear orgasm."

"It was a damn fucking good orgasm," I say in agreement. "Oh, and the lasagna was awesome, too."

I roll to my side, facing her. Lifting to an elbow, I rest my head in the palm of my hand. My eyes slowly travel down her body, trailing a finger right along with my gaze. Down the center of her chest, over her stomach, and right down to the closely cropped curls guarding her sex. The curls are darker, glistening with her juices and my cum. I push a finger right down in between, grazing over her clit, which causes her to groan before I push my digit inside of her. I feel her muscles contract all around me before I pull my now-soaked finger out.

I rub it around her clit lazily while I stare at what I'm doing. Rachel moans, swivels her hips, and curses under her breath. I ignore her, fascinated with how responsive her body is to me even though she just came spectacularly moments ago. I press against her clit harder, rub a little faster. Rachel's breath comes out in choppy little pants.

"Fuck," she barks as her hips shoot off the bed. It catches me by surprise since I didn't think she'd come that fast, but I slip a finger back inside and sure as shit, her muscles ripple all around me as the orgasm takes control of her body.

She lets out a huge huff of relief as she sags back down into the mattress. I pull my finger out, giving a tiny flick to her clit before bringing my hand back up to rest across the lower part of her stomach.

My gaze travels up to her face, which is flushed and sweaty. She glares at me, which I find comical. She fucking enjoyed that as much as I did.

But then I notice something. I glide my palm over her belly and muse almost, "Is it me, or are you beginning to show?"

Rachel's head lifts from the pillow, and she looks down at her stomach. "I thought I was just feeling a little bloated, but… maybe."

I lift my hand, and we stare at her abdomen.

And yes… it's got the tiniest, most barely perceptible pooch to it.

"Now that, Miss Hart, is sexy as fuck," I say, looking back to her with a grin.

She rolls her eyes. "You won't be saying that when I'm waddling around, all fat and miserable."

"Now there you're just wrong," I assure her. "Knowing it's our kid in there, I'm going to be turned on and horny as shit the entire time."

"Well, that's good," she quips. "Because I'm perpetually horny."

"It's me, right? Not the hormones." I waggle my

brows.

"Sure, baby," she says, lifting a hand to pat me condescendingly on the cheek. "If that's what you want to believe."

"Let's put that to the test," I tell her with a low growl. I capture her hand in mine, dragging it down my body. I force her fingers to wrap around my dick, which should be spent and utterly happy right now. It jumps at her touch and I squeeze my hand around hers, causing her to squeeze me. "Return the favor I just gave you. Hand only."

Rachel's eyes go from glacial blue to a dark indigo. She sucks in a harsh breath in between her nostrils, pulling her bottom lip in between her teeth. Rolling toward me, she starts to stroke my cock and I let my hold on her hand go.

"That's not pregnancy hormones," I murmur, holding back a groan of appreciation as she jacks me. "That's all you, wanting to get me off."

She doesn't argue.

Just rolls further into me so she can press her lips to the base of my throat. She kisses and licks at me, all the while stroking my dick with the perfect amount of pressure and speed. I've never been one for hand jobs. Rather have a mouth on me, but fuck if this doesn't feel just as good as when she was just fucking me.

And I'm not ashamed to admit that.

It's all Rachel.

My cock goes fully hard and in no time, Rachel's jerking me frantically. My balls tighten with an impending orgasm, and without any real thought, I bat Rachel's hand away. I roll on top of her, take my cock in hand, and shove it inside of her still-wet pussy.

She screams, clawing at my back, and I explode inside of her. My head drops to her shoulder, and I groan deeply as I fill her back up again. I can't get her any more pregnant than she is, but fuck if I don't like my cum inside of her.

I roll back off, flop to my back, and take some deep breaths to get my heart rate back under control. She's the one who now rolls toward me, elbow to mattress and head in her hand.

She grins down at me in triumph. "That was hot as hell."

"You give excellent hand jobs," I tell her with a return smirk.

"I like you coming inside of me," she says, her voice going soft and breathy. Her hand strokes down my chest, to my stomach, and finally grazes along my softening dick that I'm pretty sure will be dead for a while. Still, I love the touch of her on me, even if it's just with post-fucking affection.

"You ready for our visit next week?" she asks, and all thoughts of sex are forgotten.

Exactly a week from today, we see Dr. Anchors as Rachel will be close to the end of her first trimester. I had been tentatively scheduled to do security detail for a politician flying into Vegas, but Kynan easily replaced me so I could go with Rachel.

"I am." I cover her hand with mine, pulling it up to hold against my chest. I turn to face her on the bed. "But nothing fun is going to happen."

Rachel laughs. I'm going crazy waiting for the first ultrasound, but that won't happen until she's at least sixteen weeks. Dr. Anchors didn't think it was medically necessary on her first visit since she was in such great health with no risk factors other than her age of thirty-five.

"We have to decide if we want to do the amniocentesis," she says as she glances down to where our hands are interlocked. I expect her to pull away from me at any time, because Rachel's never been big into affection or post-coitus snuggling.

She doesn't, though.

"*You* have to decide," I say with emphasis. "That's totally up to you. Fuck if I'd want a damn needle stuck in my belly like that."

Giving my hand a squeeze, she says, "I'd do it if you want me to. I think he said the time to do it would be between fourteen and sixteen weeks."

Her eyes search mine, perhaps trying to discern my true feelings, but I know what they are. "It isn't necessary, Rachel. Even if it showed abnormalities, I'd still want the baby."

A tenderness I'd never seen before takes over her entire face, and her hand squeezes mine again but doesn't relax. It grips me tightly, and her smile is soft. "Yeah... I know that about you. You'd want the baby no matter what. But would you like to know so we can be prepared?"

I don't bother pointing out to her that she said "we" instead of "you". She almost makes it sound like a team effort after the birth, but I think that was merely a slip of her tongue.

However, she brings up a good point. If we knew there was a problem ahead of time, we could at least be better prepared to welcome him or her into the world.

So the baby could have every need met.

"Maybe we should," I muse.

"We should," she says confidently. "I don't like the unknown."

CHAPTER 16

Rachel

I PULL MY shirt down before running my fingers through my wet hair, which is the most attention it will get right now. Besides, it always looks best when I just let it naturally dry.

After putting my sweat-soaked clothes in my gym duffel, I close my locker and rotate the combo. Only thing left is to put on fresh socks and my tennis shoes, and then I have to head across town to meet Bodie at Dr. Anchors' office.

Sal walks into the locker room, a towel wrapped around his sweaty neck. He'd been in the gym lifting by himself, and we just quietly disregarded each other while I was working out. The gym is usually empty in the afternoons, most of us preferring to get our workouts in early. Today I was sidelined with some nausea when I woke up. By the time I was feeling better, I had time for just a quick run and a short kettle bell workout.

Sal's eyes lock with mine, and he gives me a nod in

greeting.

"Sal," I respond back politely.

I pull my first sock on while Sal opens his locker, which is just three down from mine. When he closes it, holding a shave kit and a fresh towel in hand, he surprises me by sitting down on the opposite end of the bench from where I'm sitting.

"What's up?" I ask while I put my other sock on.

"I wanted to say I'm sorry," he says gruffly. "For questioning you."

I shrug, not wanting to make a big deal of it. "It was legit."

"No, actually… it wasn't. You know I've got no qualms with the fact you're a woman, Hart. You know I'd gladly march into battle with you. I should have trusted you when you said you were capable despite the pregnancy. I shouldn't have doubted you."

I freeze with my sock halfway on my foot, my mouth dropping slightly in disbelief. Sal's not the type to admit he's wrong, so this is big.

"You know I'm old school," he continues, which spurs me to finish putting on my sock. I drop my leg to the floor and listen. "And I think that just sort of came out badly. But when I stepped back, and thought about all the things we've been through over the years, I realized I trusted you to tell us the truth if you couldn't do your job. I know you'd never put any of us in harm's way, just so you could keep doing what you love."

Yes, I'll admit... some of it might be hormonal, but the genuine rush of affection and care I feel toward Sal right this moment overwhelms me. I have to struggle not to leap on him and give him a big bear hug.

"Thank you," I tell him, the sincerity and rush of gratitude making my voice quaver. "That means a lot because I respect you so much as a teammate."

Sal's face is usually hard and intimidating, but it softens tremendously. "And I'll try to not tease you so much... seeing as how you're all hormonal and everything."

I lean across the expanse of the bench and punch him hard in his right pec. He's so fucking built, though, my knuckles ache.

He just laughs at me, pulls his sweaty towel from around his neck, and mops at his face. When he's looking at me again, his expression sobers. "But still...I know this is hard for you. Your life is getting ready to drastically change, and I know motherhood is going to cut in on your work at Jameson."

My face immediately flushes hot with embarrassment as I realize... this is the first person outside of Kynan and Jerico who has mentioned what happens after the birth. Sal just assumes I'm going to be involved, and if ever there was a time I've doubted my decision, it's now. Because no matter how progressive my teammates are regarding me being a woman on the team, there's still the expectation I'm going to raise the baby.

When that expectation is not met, I'm going to look like a total douche to my Jameson family, and yes... that embarrasses me. For the first time, I consider perhaps leaving Jameson after the birth and starting a new life somewhere.

In a place where people won't know I abandoned my baby because not only was I not ready to be a mom, but also because I was terrified that I wouldn't be a good mom. Being a mother meant a commitment and responsibility I'd never been quite able to handle. It's why I've never had a serious relationship before, and I just know inherently I'd be bad at it.

"That's a totally and seriously fucked-up look on your face right now, Hart," Sal observes, and I raise my head, blinking at him stupidly.

But I can't lie, because the truth will come out eventually. The whole "Bodie taking the baby to Nebraska" will make it quite clear to everyone.

I pick at the shoestrings on my tennis shoe sitting on the bench, refusing to look at Sal. "Um... I'm actually not going to raise the baby."

I look up tentatively to find Sal staring at me in shock.

"Then who is?" he practically stammers. It never even occurs to him that it would be the father.

"Bodie," I tell him after a hard swallow, which is nothing more than me trying to push down the knot of shame that's threatening to come up. "He's going to go home to Nebraska so his parents can help him."

Sal whistles low and shakes his head. "Damn, Hart. Talk about gender-role reversals."

I raise my chin a little and give the same spiel I'd given Kynan and Jerico. "I'm just not ready to give up my career."

Sal tells me something I already know, because Kynan and Jerico both told me the same thing. "You wouldn't have to give it up. Who said you couldn't be a mother and a badass mercenary? I mean... plenty of women go off to war and leave their kids back home with their husbands. This is the twenty-first century, Hart. You need to move into it."

My head bows down not in shame, but in frustration. Yes, I know this. He's right. Kynan's right. Jerico is right. I can totally keep doing this job and be a mother, particularly with Bodie raising the baby right beside me. I can't use that as an excuse anymore, and that leaves me feeling off balance and panicky.

I'm not overly close to Sal. We have a mutually respectful working relationship and a trusted bond that we'd protect the other. But we don't hang out as friends, and we've never had a meaningful discussion unless an argument we once had over the best whey protein powder on the market counts.

So, I'm totally surprised at myself when I look back up to him and blurt out, "I don't think I can be a mom."

Sal's chin jerks inward and his eyebrows rise high.

"Shut the fuck up, Hart. You can totally be a mom."

The feelings of panic and desperation start to constrict my chest. I shake my head, my voice almost shrill. "No, I can't. What do I know about being a mom? I'm hard and no nonsense. If my kid fell and scraped his knee, I'd tell him to get up and rub some dirt in it. I am not mother material."

Rather than empathize, Sal laughs. Literally throws his head back and laughs from deep in his gut. When he finally looks at me, it's with gentle reproach as he shakes his head. "You're totally equipped to be a mom. You're loyal and dedicated. You'd protect your kid's life with your own, and you'd never let anything bad happen to it. You'd give it the best opportunities, sacrificing yourself to do so. You'd be calm and steady and completely unflappable. That's all great mother material, and do you know how I know you got it?"

I ignore the slight ringing in my ears that started when he told me I could be a mom, giving a stupid shake of my head.

Sal leans closer, his voice soft. "I know it because you exhibit all those things to our teammates at Jameson. There's no one stronger than you. No bigger advocate. No greater confidant. Never a more loyal person to those she's sworn to protect. You're more a mom than most women out there, Hart. And you can take that to the bank."

"I'm not good at commitment," I whisper, throwing

out another tactic in hopes Sal will take back everything he just said.

"Are you talking about the baby or Bodie now?" Sal asks dryly.

I jerk backward, surprised by his question. Surely, he knows I'm talking about the baby, right?

But admittedly, the rise of fear that swelled within me at the mention of Bodie's name is probably an indication I'm thinking about him, too.

I don't answer him directly, instead saying, "It's casual between Bodie and me. That's all."

"Bullshit," he says with resounding confidence. "What I've seen of you and Bodie, and I've seen quite a bit at The Wicked Horse, it's anything but casual."

"We're fucking in a sex club," I growl.

"You're sharing intense, intimate experiences at a sex club with him and exclusively him," he retorts. "That's not casual."

"He's too young." I'm grasping at straws now, and I know the nine-year age difference between us is probably lame.

"Again, bullshit. He's a good dude with a wise head on his shoulders. I mean, if you're all vain and worrying about getting wrinkles before him, fine then. But you and I both know you're not vain, Hart."

Sal crosses his arms over his chest, looking down at me with superiority.

Asshole.

The door to the locker room opens, and Cage walks in dressed in a pair of khaki shorts and a white tank top. He's got on flip-flops, a ball cap with shades perched on top, and his gym bag slung over his shoulder. He gives us both a nod and walks over to the next row of lockers.

Sal leans across the bench again and murmurs, "Rachel... you don't have to make any decisions right now. Think about it. Take your time. You've got a while before that baby comes."

My eyes cut toward the lockers because I know if I look at him, he'll take that as an acknowledgment he's right. I have no business declaring my intentions this early, when I know damn well I've been mired under second thoughts nearly every day.

I stay stubbornly silent, but Sal isn't done with me. "If you commit to that baby, that means Bodie can stay, too. Doing a job he loves."

My head snaps back to Sal, and I narrow my eyes. "Isn't it enough I'm carrying this baby for him? Now I have to give up my life, so he can have his career, too?"

Sal stands from the bench and chuckles. Giving a shake of his head, his eyes glimmer with sage wisdom. "That's the thing, Hart. Having a kid isn't about giving up your life. It's about having a better, more complete life. You'll be gaining far more than you'll ever give up."

I grind my teeth, knowing if I try to continue arguing with him, I'll probably end up screaming with bitter frustration. These are decisions I never wanted to be faced with, and there are many people this is going to affect.

"I'm gonna jump in the shower," Sal says as he steps over the bench. "Just think about things, okay?"

"Yeah, sure," I mutter, just so he'll leave and I can be done with this.

I sit there for a few moments, staring blankly at my tennis shoes. Finally, I glance at my watch and see I have to get going to make my doctor's appointment.

I quickly get on one shoe, then another. Picking my gym bag up, I head toward the exit. Just as I make it past the end of the lockers, I'm brought up short by Cage, who steps in front of me.

Startled, I curse at him. "Fuck. You scared me."

He gives me a tight smile and leans against the edge of the locker, folding his arms across his chest. "Didn't mean to eavesdrop, but you and Sal were loud enough that I couldn't help it."

My body locks tight, not only because Cage is getting ready to get into my business, but also because his allegiance is to Bodie as his best friend. I can tell by the look on his face that what he's going to say isn't going to be nice.

"Don't fuck with his heart," Cage says in what can only be termed a menacing tone.

"Why would I fuck with his heart?" I ask sarcastically. I mean… it's my heart I've been focused on, knowing it was going to break at some point in the future.

"You wouldn't do it intentionally." His tone is bland

and unenthused. "But you're so focused on yourself and the decision you have in front of you. I don't want you to lose sight of the fact that Bodie cares about you."

This isn't a surprise. Of course I know Bodie cares for me. If there was ever any doubt, it was put to rest when he ordered me to go to bed while pirates were attacking the ship. He was worried about me, and couldn't be effective.

Worried.

About me.

My fingers rub at the bridge of my nose. I let my eyes close in a brief moment of respite from Cage's accusing look before I let out a sigh and open my eyes. "I won't hurt him. I care about him, too."

"Yeah," Cage says softly... in agreement with me. But then his tone hardens, "But not enough. Make it so you care about him enough so you make a better effort *not* to hurt him. Either go all in or cut him loose, but this in-between shit spells disaster."

A lump forms in my throat that has nothing to do with shame or anger. Instead, it's a knot formed from cold hard truth. I've let myself get close to Bodie. He's come to care for me, and me for him. But I keep that barrier up, knowing I can't give much more without sacrificing my own heart.

I also know that's not fair to Bodie.

Swallowing, I level my eyes on Cage's. "I won't hurt him."

CHAPTER 17

Bodie

I PURPOSELY WAIT until eight PM to call my parents. I'd come home after our appointment with Dr. Anchors, riding high on the thrill of an ultrasound we hadn't expected. It only came about because I was bitching and moaning having to wait another four weeks, and Dr. Anchors had laughed at me.

"We're actually going to do a vaginal ultrasound today," he told us, and I had a zing of pure electrical excitement flow through me. "We really only use it in higher risk situations or to pinpoint conception date, but you're pretty clear on the date it happened. Still, let's check your baby's heartbeat out."

And then he did.

It was amazing. While he gently circled a wand inside of Rachel, I practically leaned all the way across her on the examination table to get my face as close as possible to the screen. Rachel sort of grunted and pushed at me, but then I grabbed her hand and squeezed so hard she let me be.

I couldn't tell what the fuck I was seeing, but we heard the heartbeat. So fast and strong.

"It's a girl," I declared.

Rachel rolled her eyes, and Dr. Anchors told me we'd find that out hopefully at sixteen weeks. On a more sobering note, we told Dr. Anchors we wanted the amniocentesis, and that's scheduled to take place at the same time.

Still, when I walked in my house, I was riding high on the first tangible proof that there is something growing inside of Rachel that belongs to me. There was no way I could keep this from my parents anymore, and while I am not looking forward to leaving Jameson Group and all my friends and teammates, I am so looking forward to my kid.

I walk into my kitchen and sit down at the small, round table that seats four. I got it at a garage sale. The legs are uneven, so it wobbles when I rest my arms on top. Tapping on the icon for FaceTime, I dial my mom's cell and wait. My heart is thumping madly, both terrified and excited to share the news with my parents.

My mom's beautiful face appears on the screen, and I can see she's in the kitchen. I figured she'd just be finishing up the dishes from supper, which is why I waited until now to call.

She blows a breath of air up to push her bangs back and grins at me. "FaceTime? Now that's a nice treat. You look good, sweet boy."

I rub my face along the jawline, feeling the scrape of stubble on my face. Of course my mom would say that.

"You look better," I tell her with a wink. "When are you going to leave Dad and find yourself a young hottie?"

My mom blushes, and I hear my dad in the background say, "I heard that."

Then his face pushes into the range of the camera on her phone. While my mom still has a youthful face barely marred by wrinkles or time, my dad's face is weathered from countless hours out in the sun working the farm. He started wearing a beard a few years ago, and it's shot through liberally with a steel gray against his dark hair. But his eyes are a light hazel, sparkling with the inner youth of a man who is as strong as an ox and could probably still whoop my ass.

"Hi, Dad," I say with a grin.

Mom nudges Dad to the side to take up more of the camera. "Guess what? Millie Perkins got elected Mayor of North Platte."

I went to high school with Millie's daughter, Samantha. I also know this is a lead in.

"And Samantha's moved back home," she says with a sly smile. "She looks fabulous."

"Not interested, Mom," I chide. She's forever trying to set me up, as if a pretty girl would get me to come running home.

A pretty girl would not.

A baby would.

"So, I actually have something important to talk to you both about, and wanted to do it face to face, so a video chat was the next best thing."

Both of their faces pinch tight with immediate concern, so I rush to reassure them. "It's not bad."

My dad's face relaxes, but my mother's does not. She leans in closer to the camera. "Lay it on us. We can handle anything as a family."

"It's not bad, Mom," I drawl with an amused shake of my head. "I promise."

Dad chuckles, but Mom doesn't look convinced.

I take a deep breath. "Okay… there's just no good way to lead into this, so I'm just going to say it, and then you can ask questions. I got a woman pregnant, and I'm going to be a dad."

My dad's eyes bug out of his head, but my mom's turn soft and tender. She's already imagining all the ways to spoil her newest grandchild.

"Oh, honey," she murmurs. She tilts her head to the side, and her eyes fill with tears. "That's wonderful. You'll make a wonderful father. Won't he, Geo?"

She turns to look at my dad, but he's all about the business of how this happened. "Who is this girl? And are you going to get married?"

I give a slow shake of my head, trying to brace myself against the disappointment I know I'll get from my mother. "Actually no. It was an accident. Not planned. And um... well, we're not really together."

"What do you mean 'not really together'?" my dad asks with a cocked eyebrow.

"I mean we have no intentions of being a couple together in the future." It's the first and simplest thing that comes to mind.

"Which means you're together now," my dad concludes, and I cringe internally. He's making this complicated.

"What we have is casual and has an expiration date to it," I clip out.

"It sounds like there's something cryptic within that statement I'm missing," my dad presses.

I let out a gust of frustrated air and rub my hand over the top of my head. This is the part I've been dreading, because I know my kind, decent midwestern farming parents won't understand. "Rachel... the baby's mother... doesn't want to raise it. I do. So, I'm going to be leaving Jameson and coming home after the baby is born. That's what I mean by an expiration date."

My mom's face crumbles, not for any reason other than she's assuming I'm heartbroken over this turn of events. My mother, the romantic, probably believes that love created this baby and our love isn't going to survive the circumstances.

"Listen," I say quickly to make them understand, and because I don't want them disliking Rachel from the start. "Rachel is an amazing woman. She's one of my teammates at Jameson, and we sort of got stupid one night and this happened. She could have easily chosen an abortion… could have kept this hidden from me. But she didn't, and she agreed to carry the baby. Just because she's not ready to be a mom yet doesn't make her a bad woman. I totally respect her decision."

I hate it, but I respect it.

I hate it because I think she's making the wrong decision. Not for me, but for her. I think she's going to have terrible regrets one day, and I'd spare her that pain if I could. But I can't tell her what to do. She has to figure it out for herself.

I also hate it because I do care about her. I could see us really having something solid together as a couple. Over the past several weeks, I've come to know the real Rachel, and she's a generously giving woman. She has so much to offer our kid. Fuck… I want what she has to potentially offer to me if I can ever figure out how to knock down the rest of her reticent barriers.

"Bodie," my mom says, drawing me out of my thoughts. "Come home. We'd love it so much if you did that. I'll help you. You can work the farm until you decide what you want to do."

My throat tightens because this is it. This is where I commit to a whole new life for myself.

"I'd like that too," I tell her.

And I would. I'd like it, but I wouldn't love it. While

there is nothing nearer to my heart than my family, farm life is never what I wanted. Nebraska is never what I wanted.

♦

THERE'S A KNOCK on my door, rousing me from sleep. I rub at my eyes, pick up my phone from the coffee table where I'd laid it, and look at the time.

12:37 AM.

There's another knock—three short raps that have me pushing up from the couch. I pad to the door and can see Rachel standing on the other side through the panes of glass. Her face is softly illuminated by the yellow glow of the porch light, and it strikes me how ethereal her beauty is at times. So different than the tough, badass woman I'm used to.

I pull the door open. "Hey. Come on in."

She pushes by me, spins around, and accuses. "You didn't come to the club tonight."

I scratch at the back of my head and give her a hangdog look. I hadn't promised her I would when she texted me a few hours ago, only that I'd try to make it.

It's the first time I've bailed on her invitation, but after talking to my parents tonight, I honestly just didn't feel like it. My talk with them had brought me down low, a potent reminder that my life as I loved it was over.

My career that brought me utter joy was done.

Sure… I was getting something great in return, but I

was losing so much of my identity. So what if it made me a little melancholy?

"Sorry," I mutter. "Just was tired tonight."

Rachel cocks a perfectly shaped eyebrow into a higher arch. "Bullshit. What's wrong?"

With a sigh, I turn away and head back to my couch. I flop down on one end, throwing my arm over the back. She walks silently toward me, taking a seat at the opposite end.

"What's wrong?" she repeats, this time in a softer, more concerned tone.

I stare at her a moment, wondering if I should even share with her. I mean… we are nothing more than just fuck buddies, right?

"Bodie," she murmurs. "Talk to me."

That right there strikes at me deep. The tone in her voice that tells me she's concerned.

"I talked to my parents tonight," I say, rubbing at the stubble on my chin.

Her eyes grow soft with empathy. "And they're upset?"

My smile is weak. "On the contrary… they couldn't be more thrilled. Me coming home with a baby in tow. My mother's dreams are being totally fulfilled."

Rachel has always had an expressive face when she chooses to show what she's thinking, and I can read her loud and clear. She knows I don't want to leave Jameson. She knows I'm cutting a part of myself away by doing so and returning home.

And she knows it's her fault for not stepping up to the plate to be a mother.

"Don't even look at me like that," I say as I lean across and take her hand. "Your choices have nothing to do with me. And I spent a great deal of time telling my parents how much I admire you for giving of yourself so I can have this baby. I'm good, Rachel."

To my surprise, Rachel scrambles across the couch and pushes herself onto my lap. She loops her arms around my neck and rests her head on my chest. "I wish I were braver. I wish I could grab onto this the way you have."

I bring my hand to the back of her head, stroking a thumb over her hair and just holding her to me. "You're one of the bravest people I know. Making the decision to follow your heart… to keep your career. That's a brave decision, Rachel."

She makes a sound deep in her throat that tells me she doesn't believe a word I'm saying. But I don't try to press the point home, because frankly, I want Rachel really thinking about this.

Again, it goes back to regrets. I'm afraid she's going to have massive ones, and one thing I've come to learn about this woman is that when she goes all into something, she puts her soul on the line. I'm afraid her soul is going to get crushed when she realizes one day what she's lost.

Rising from the couch, I cradle Rachel in my arms and walk back to my bedroom. "No more talking," I tell her. "We have better things to do."

Rachel lifts her head slightly to press her lips to my throat. She doesn't say anything, just nods in agreement, and that's good enough for right now.

CHAPTER 18

Rachel

MY EYES FLUTTER open. For a moment, I'm completely disoriented. Then I take in the warm body behind me and the arm locked around my stomach.

I feel Bodie's breath on my shoulder. Strong and steady.

Just like Bodie.

Most of our hookups have been at The Wicked Horse, but last night was a bit different. When he asked me to stay, I didn't feel compelled to run.

A rumble in my belly has me taking stock of the morning situation. No nausea, which is happening less frequently, and a full bladder.

That means bathroom first and raiding Bodie's fridge second. Maybe I'll cook us breakfast.

When I roll out of bed, I'm surprised to see it's close to 9:30. I never sleep that late, but then again, Bodie and I didn't get a lot of rest last night either. The memories make me smile, and I reconsider waking Bodie up with my mouth before eggs and bacon.

Bodie's house only has one bathroom set between the two bedrooms. It's small, and the decor and fixtures date back to the 80s. Because we make such good money, most of the people at Jameson spend their money on fancy houses, cars, or other toys. Not Bodie, though.

He drives a truck that's probably at least five years old, and this house is nothing to write home about. I'm not surprised. He just doesn't seem like a frivolous guy, but that's not to say he won't throw money around. Him paying two thousand for us to have use of the room at The Wicked Horse speaks volumes.

I'd thrown one of Bodie's t-shirts on in the early morning hours after the last time we fucked, as well as slipped my panties back on. I'm totally comfortable in my nudity, but for whatever reason, I've never felt comfortable sleeping without some clothes on. Bodie teased me about it while he stayed completely naked when we finally decided to get some sleep. He told me that was the "soldier" in me, always wanting to be ready should danger sneak up and catch me unawares.

I hike Bodie's t-shirt up since it swallows me, and then pull my panties down. As I sit on the toilet, still a little groggy from the heavy and very comfortable sleep I had in his arms, my gaze lands on the crotch of my underwear that's stretched between my knees.

It takes me a moment to understand what I'm looking at, but once I do, I can't control the piercing shriek that comes out of my mouth.

"Bodie!"

I hastily grab toilet paper and wipe, my heart absolutely shriveling as it comes away with some light pink blood on it. Same color as the tiny spots in my panties.

Bodie comes crashing into the bathroom, still naked and hair sticking up all over the place. "What's wrong?"

I open my mouth, but nothing comes out. I just hold up the toilet paper and then look down to my panties while I stupidly sit on the toilet.

His keen eyes take it all in, and when his gaze lands on my panties, he hisses through his teeth. "Shit."

I can feel panic starting to rise, but then Bodie is gently pulling me up from the toilet. I toss the tissue in as Bodie squats to pull my panties up.

"Okay... we're not going to panic. Dr. Anchors said some light spotting is normal in the first trimester. Is this the first time you've seen blood?"

I'm completely mute so I just nod.

"Okay," he says. This time, there's an air of calm confidence in his tone. He takes me by the elbow and leads me to the bedroom. "Here's what we're going to do. We're going to get dressed and drive to Dr. Anchors' office. I'll call on the way there."

He releases his hold on me and starts to efficiently walk around and pick up our clothes. He hands me mine and has to give me a gentle push. "Get dressed, Rachel."

I finally move, the urgency of the situation penetrating the fog of my panicked thoughts. I manage to get dressed. By the time I'm tying my shoe laces, Bodie's standing by the door with his keys in his hand.

When I reach him, his hands go to my shoulders and he peers down at me. "Rachel... I'm sure everything is fine, okay?"

I nod, still not able to speak. All I can think about is China... gushing blood and horrible cramps and...

"Rachel," Bodie says a little louder, and I blink at him. "It will be okay."

I hear him.

I even understand him.

He's telling me that no matter what happens, it's going to be okay. It's a lovely sentiment, but one that he's so very wrong about. This is the biggest reason I've been so stressed about this pregnancy, because I was afraid I'd do something to ruin it.

What if this is because I went to Singapore? Or maybe it's the way I train and workout? Maybe I'm not eating the right types of food, or what if... what if it's because of all the fucking I've been doing with Bodie? We've been exuberant to say the least.

"You hear me?" Bodie asks, getting so close our noses are almost touching.

I finally give a tiny cough, clear the fear from my throat, and whisper, "Okay."

"Good," he says before leaning in and pressing his

lips to my forehead. "Now let's go see what's happening."

Bodie does an admirable job getting us to the doctor's office. Even though he's giving me an air of calm, I can tell by the way he pushes the speed limit and runs questionable yellow lights that he's worried.

When I tell the receptionist what's going on, we're immediately ushered into an exam room. Within five minutes, Dr. Anchors is there.

"Rachel... Bodie," he says as he walks in and goes straight to the sink. I'm already in a gown and on the examination table, ready to throw my feet in the stirrups. "I understand you have some spotting."

"It was in my underwear this morning," I say. To my embarrassment, Bodie grabs my panties from my pile of clothes and shows it to the doctor.

Dr. Anchors leans over and examines the blood while he puts gloves on. "Is that all?"

"Some on the toilet paper after I peed this morning," I choke out. "About the same amount, I think."

"All right, Rachel. Let's get you in the stirrups. I'm going to have a look." His voice is like Bodie's. Composed. Relaxed. Positive.

It doesn't calm me down at all, and I can feel my heartbeat ringing in my ears. My blood pressure was high when we came in, but the nurse took it again after I laid on the table, and it started to come down a little. She assured me it was probably stress.

I get in the stirrups and brace while Dr. Anchors gives me an examination. He even pulls a wand with a light attached to the table and shines it up inside. Surprisingly, he doesn't spend a lot of time down there.

When he pulls back, he says, "I don't see any cervical polyps, which can often be a source of spotting since they can get agitated from increased estrogen. But doesn't mean there wasn't one that was bleeding, but isn't right now."

He pulls his gloves off, and I take my feet out of the stirrups. Bodie helps me to sit up on the table.

When Dr. Anchors turns around, he asks, "Any cramping? Pain? Extra nausea?"

"No," I say with a shake of my head. "I feel fine."

"Well, spotting can come from many sources. It could have been from the vaginal ultrasound we did yesterday. It could come from sex, especially if it's vigorous."

Bodie and I exchange guilty looks.

"Let's do another vaginal ultrasound just to check the heartbeat. As long as that looks good, there's really nothing to do."

"Bed rest?" Bodie asks. I nod my head up and down enthusiastically over this suggestion. I'll sit on my ass in a bed for the next five months if I have to.

Dr. Anchors chuckles. "Most likely not. Let's see what the ultrasound shows, and then we'll make a plan."

♦

BODIE AND I walk out of Dr. Anchors' office, our hands clasped tightly together. I'm not sure at what point we joined them together, but it feels natural and necessary. We walk silently to his truck.

My heart rate has come down somewhat, and while I don't have the panic of impending grief bubbling inside of me, I'm still not quite assured.

Even though Dr. Anchors did his best to make us feel better. The baby's heartbeat is strong. There are many benign things that could cause spotting. Like he said... polyps, sex, the ultrasound wand. He told us that spotting of that amount was really not something to be worried about, but that I should take it easy for a few days and keep watch. He told me to return or go to the emergency room if I started cramping or bleeding heavily.

He gave me a pointed look when he described what he meant by heavy bleeding, because he knows I know exactly what that means since I've miscarried before.

"You okay?" Bodie asks as we reach the passenger side of his truck.

"Not really," I reply glumly. "That scared the shit out of me."

"Me too," he admits and for the first time, he allows me to see how this affected him. Prior to this moment, he was a rock. Solid to the core and exhibiting all the strength that would be needed for the worst news we could potentially get.

Bodie releases my hand to open the door, but I don't turn to get in. Instead, I look down at the pavement for a moment before I get up the nerve to look him in the eye. "Can I... um... think I can stay with you for a few days or you stay at my house? Just in case... you know... something happens?"

"Fuck yes," Bodie says on an expelled breath of relief that I'd ask such a thing. "Of course. I'm not going to leave you alone. Would you prefer to stay at my house or yours?"

"Mine if that's okay with you?" My voice is whisper soft. Fatigued even.

"Then that's what we'll do," he says as he takes my elbow to help me in the truck.

We go back to Bodie's house, and it takes him all of ten minutes to pack up a bag that will get him through the next few days. He's set to go on a security detail on Monday, but that's five days away. We agreed if all was fine with me, he'd go.

At my house, Bodie asks me if I'm hungry and surprisingly, I am. He takes charge of my kitchen and makes us breakfast. It's just a simple scrambled eggs and bacon meal, but I find myself so thoroughly drained from the stress of this morning that I do nothing more than sit at my kitchen island and watch him work.

While we eat, I take stock of the last few hours. I pay

particular attention to the range of emotions that totally played havoc on me, and I realize something very, very important.

The depth of fear I felt today is the clearest of indications that I am attached to this baby. That knowledge is troubling, because it means my decisions have to be reevaluated. When I told Bodie I'd carry the baby and then he could raise it, it was because I hadn't felt much in the way of a bond. But that's certainly not the case now. I'm not even sure when it happened, or if it's just been building, but I knew I was in for a big spiral downward if I lost the baby today.

"What's wrong?" Bodie asks softly, and I look up at him. When I do, I feel a tear run down my cheek and realize I'm crying.

I drop my fork, and it clatters on the table. Pressing my face into my hands, I take a shuddering breath. I can hear Bodie's chair scrape along the floor, and then he's squatting by me.

When he gently pulls my hands away, I'm forced to look at his warm brown eyes filled with abject worry.

"What's wrong?" he repeats again.

I dash my tears away and suck in air through my nose. When I let it out, I bring Bodie into my circle of trust. "I've been pregnant before. And I miscarried. It was thirteen years ago."

"Oh, Rachel," Bodie breathes out with so much sorrow I can barely stand it. He takes my hands in his, and gives me a gentle squeeze. "I'm so sorry."

For a moment, I'm confused. I expected him to be angry upon learning this, but he just stares at me with open acceptance of my history.

"I'm sorry I didn't tell you earlier," I say with a sniffle. "I was so afraid it was a bad omen for this pregnancy, and I didn't want to worry you. But I did tell Dr. Anchors about it."

"When you asked to speak to him privately on that first visit," he concludes.

"Yeah. He told me that a single miscarriage does not increase odds of another."

Bodie gives me a bright smile. "See... nothing to worry about."

I give a hard shake to my head. "I thought it was my fault. Still do to some extent even though doctors—Dr. Anchors included—have told me it wasn't."

"Why would you think it was?"

I take another deep breath. "I was living wild and dangerous. Doing stupid shit. I had just jumped off a tower in China and then miscarried later that day. I didn't even know I was pregnant."

"Jesus," Bodie murmurs, and then he's scooping me up out of the chair. I don't protest. I'm not sure if it makes me weak or not, but I lay my head on his shoulder while he carries me into the living room.

He drops down onto the couch, keeping me on his lap. He cradles me like a child, and fresh tears swamp my eyes.

"Rachel?" Bodie murmurs with a question implicit in his tone. "Did the father of the child make you feel like it was your fault or something?"

I shake my head, giving an involuntarily sniffle. "He didn't even know. I wasn't with him all that long, and we broke up before for unrelated things."

"Okay," he says with relief, assured that some other asshole hadn't put those thoughts in my head.

It's so very strange. I know without a doubt had I miscarried today, Bodie would have never made me feel like shit. He told me it would all be okay no matter what, and built within that statement is a deep trust I have in him that it would—eventually—be okay.

He was so amazing today. Putting aside his own fears to be strong for me. To help make me strong.

No one has ever done that for me before.

"I've never been in a serious relationship before," I tell him while pressing my cheek to his chest. His one arm supports my back, the other stroking my thigh in a calming way. "I've never been good on committing to a person. Accepting the responsibility that comes with such a commitment."

"Think I figured that one out on my own," Bodie says dryly, and it makes me chuckle.

"It's why I don't think I'd be a good mom," I admit softly.

Bodie's entire body jerks and he rears back so he can

look down at me. I tilt my face up to his, surprised to see anger there. "Just because you've never been in love with a man before doesn't mean you wouldn't love your child, Rachel. Those are two totally separate things."

"I was so scared this morning when I saw that blood," I admit. I lay it all out. "I didn't want to lose this baby. I don't know what that means. It's contrary to what I thought I wanted."

Bodie adjusts his body, shifting me slightly on his lap so we can look directly at each other. His eyes roam over my face for a moment, as if he's collecting the right words to say. Finally... when he says them... they hit me hard.

"Rachel... perhaps you need to give motherhood a try. I'd be here to help you out. We could do this as a team. I'm afraid if you don't, you are going to have regrets later that could potentially destroy you. And I don't want to see that happen. More importantly, I think you would be a fantastic mother. Our child will lose so much without you in its life."

I wait for that inevitable wall to slam into place, protecting me from everything that is hard and unbearable. Yet, it doesn't come. Instead, all I can really focus on is a low-level fear deep in my belly that something is wrong with the pregnancy.

The fear causes me to feel cold from the inside out, thinking about losing this baby.

"What would that mean?" I ask curiously. "Raising

the baby as a team, I mean?"

Bodie shrugs. "We'd have to talk about it. Live together to make things easier? Live apart? Split custody? We definitely couldn't go on any ops or details together ever again. And we'd need to make sure not to go on separate ones at the same time."

That all makes sense, but that's not really satisfying my need for answers. I guess what I really want to know is what it means for us personally. Because if Bodie was going to leave with the baby to go home to Nebraska, that meant our relationship was over. But if he stays here, and we make a go at this co-parenting thing, that means that maybe we aren't over.

I had never considered a future with Bodie. It was never something that was possible. But now I'm sitting here with a man who has proven he cares about me as an individual. Who has been rock steady support to me, and has done nothing but give me happiness and pleasure.

Why would I not want to build something with him? He's the first man I've ever even considered that with.

A small voice penetrates… tells me to be cautious. The heart is a sensitive organ and can be gravely hurt. There are risks, and a relationship is hard work. I've never been cut out for it before, and I'm not sure I am now.

It's something I have to give some serious thought to, because the last thing I want to do is hurt Bodie.

But I also don't want to lose him either.

CHAPTER 19

Bodie

I BANG IMPATIENTLY on Rachel's door, completely not caring it's almost one in the morning. I came here straight from McCarran where we landed not long ago after finishing a security detail for some Saudi prince who is traveling around the United States. He attended some movie premiere in L.A., and we were hired to provide extra security coverage for him.

Rachel, of course, didn't go. The spotting incident scared the shit out of her, and even though Dr. Anchors felt the security work would be fine, she wasn't going to take any chances. She begged off, and Kynan had no problem filling her slot.

I get her fears, and truth be told, I'm glad she decided to lay low for a bit. Get past the scare, make sure everything is okay. I would have worried the whole time—same as her—and that stress can't be good either.

But this walking on eggshells is going to stop. Rachel is going a little overboard, and that ends right this fucking minute.

I bang again, and finally Rachel yells back in a sleepy, grumpy voice that comes closer to the door. "Hold your fucking horses, Wright."

So, she knows it's me at her door, even though I didn't tell her I was coming over after I landed. But really, who else would it be? Besides, she knows my patience is completely worn thin with her.

The scare with the spotting happened over ten days ago. The last three days, I'd been gone on the security detail to L.A., which meant the seven before that Rachel wouldn't let me touch her.

At all.

Okay, sure... she was fine with me staying the night, sleeping with her, and holding her in my arms. But past that, her body was off limits.

And I understood it. She was freaked, and I didn't want to make matters worse. She pointed out time and time again that Dr. Anchors said it could have been caused by sex.

I pointed out right back, "But he didn't say we couldn't have sex. Just that it could cause spotting."

But Rachel is Rachel, and I've come to learn she's stubborn. She wouldn't budge. Wouldn't even fucking let me go down on her to get her off, although I'll grudgingly admit she offered me a blow job every fucking night. I wasn't taking it, though. Not unless she was going to let me give back.

Truth be told, it was fine. I was certainly enjoying staying at her house with her. We cooked meals together, watched movies, and slept in bed wrapped totally around each other. So, it wasn't just fine. It was fucking awesome.

It's just awesome being around Rachel, and she grows softer and more accepting of my care as every day passes. Which meant I didn't grumble too much about the lack of sex.

That changed last night when I talked to her from L.A. I told her to get ready for my return, because I was going to give her an orgasm that was going to make her toes curl so tight she'd never be able to walk again.

She made a purring sound in her throat, which caused my cock to stir to life, and then killed it deader than a doornail when she said, "It's too soon."

"We'll see about that," I'd promised her ominously.

Even though I know Rachel is coming to the door, I bang two more times for posterity. She's good and pissed when she finally swings it open.

"Just what in the hell—"

She doesn't get any further because I sweep her up in my arms like a groom would his bride, and march her right back to her room. I'd like to toss her down and strip her out of her little tank top and boy shorts she's wearing, but I'm cognizant of her fears so I gently lay her down.

"We're not having sex," she sputters, but I also hear

amusement in her voice.

"Oh, yes we are," I say as I toss my phone at her. "Read it and weep."

She catches it with a perplexed look on her face, scooting back so she can lean on the pillows that are propped against the headboard. Her eyebrows draw inward as she reads the email I'd pulled up on my screen before I knocked on her door.

I've got it practically memorized because it's very short, and very sweet to me.

Dear Bodie,

My nurse informed me of your call into the office today. Attached please find the prescription you requested.

If I can be of further help, don't hesitate to contact my office.

Sincerely,
W.D. Anchors, M.D.

I pull my shirt over my head while I watch Rachel tap the screen once to pull up the attached PDF file. It's a prescription written by Dr. Anchors.

He had filled in "Rachel Hart" on the line for the patient name and dated the script for today.

Underneath, he wrote: *Sex as often as you want with no worries you are harming the baby. Don't be overzealous but have fun. Repeat as necessary.*

Rachel's eyes scan the screen, and I'm emboldened when her lips tip upward at the edges. She finally gives me a chastising look. "You bothered Dr. Anchors about this?"

"I thought you were being a little too ridiculous in your fears," I say as I strip out of my jeans. "He was only too happy to help."

She gives me a glare, but it doesn't pack any punch. I climb onto the end of the bed, then crawl my way up her body. Her legs spread slightly, and I'm sure she expects me to crawl all the way up to kiss her.

Instead, I pause and press my face into her pussy, which is covered by her sensible-looking boy shorts done in blue cotton. I inhale deeply and with such appreciation I can't help but groan.

"Oh, God," Rachel murmurs, and I can hear the defeat in her voice just from that one little move.

My head pops up, and I smile at her. She tries a reproachful look back at me, but I'm not having it. I continue my way up her body, yanking my phone from her hand and flinging it aside. Then I'm kissing her. It's a hello kiss as well as an "I'm dying to fuck you" kiss, and a kiss of just of how much I missed her the last few days.

Her fingers slide into my hair and she holds me to her tightly, her tongue sliding against mine.

Finally, I pull away and give her a sober look. "You know you don't have to do this, right? I'm just teasing you about all this. If you're not comfortable with us having sex, you can just give me a blow job."

Rachel laughs, because she knows I won't accept it unless she's getting something in return. "Just be gentle with me," she says softly but quite seriously.

"I promise," I tell her before tilting my head and pressing my lips to her jaw.

Then to her neck.

Collarbone.

Center of her chest through the material of her tank top.

Lifting my head up again, I look at her. "We'll start off very gently. Just my mouth ever so softly on your clit until you come."

Rachel cocks an eyebrow at me, then uncharacteristically becomes affectionate by sort of ruffling my hair with her hand. "You do know that the orgasms you give me are so powerful that I'm a little concerned they could rattle the baby a bit. They turn me inside out, Bodie."

I press another kiss to her chest, then look back up at her. "That may be the hottest thing you've ever said to me, Hart."

I get an eye roll, but then her hands are on my head, giving me a hard push to make me move further down her body. She's fully capitulated, and my dick is very hard and very happy in response.

When I reach those little boy shorts, which are admittedly sexy even though they cover a lot, I nip the edge with my teeth and give them a playful tug. I look up at

Rachel to find her staring at me so intently I'm stunned to inaction for a moment.

I let the cotton elastic go, and it snaps back into place. "It's the same for me," I say.

Her head tilts to the side. "What's the same?"

"The orgasms you give me are out of this world," I admit, giving her a little bit of power over me. "Never felt anything like them in my life. And do you know what?"

"What?" she whispers almost breathlessly.

"It's because there's something special between us. Call it chemical, call it emotional... I don't give a fuck what you call it. But it's something different, and I know you know it, too."

She's slow to respond, but it's what I want. She nods her head. "Yeah... it's something different. Something special."

The moment is heavy with emotion, and maybe with a little more prodding I could actually get Rachel to admit she cares for me a lot more than she's letting on. But I don't because unless Rachel gets there on her own, it will never be genuine.

So, I give her a wink and a grin. "Well, I got your special right here, baby. Spread those legs and I'll show you."

♦

Much, much later…

"HOW DO YOU feel?" I ask as I cocoon my body around her. There's something to be said for going slow and taking my time. I never knew gentleness could be so sexy, especially when Rachel became lost to pleasure and begged me to go harder.

"I feel wrecked in a good way," she murmurs in return, her voice sounding replete, happy, and drowsy all at once.

I tighten my arm slightly around her stomach, bringing her closer to my body. Sliding my hand up, I palm a breast; not for arousal but only for possessiveness. Rachel squirms to get deeper into my embrace.

"My parents are flying in Sunday for a visit," I tell her, completely expecting the total jerking of her body in surprise. "They always try to come in once a year, do a little gambling. Plus, the Fourth of July is always a good time to visit Vegas."

"Really?" she asks, her voice a little high pitched.

"They want to meet you," I continue.

Rachel squirms like a greased pig against my hold, and flips her body to face me. I rest a reassuring hand on her hip and try not to be amused by the panic on her face.

"Why do they want to meet me?" she asks fearfully.

"Relax there, Hart," I tease, dropping my hand to squeeze her ass. "They want to meet you because you're carrying their grandbaby. Because they know you're giving up a part of your life… doing something selfless to give me something, when you could have taken the easy way out. Why wouldn't they want to meet you?"

Rachel shakes her head in disbelief. "Why do you do that? Why do you make me sound like a hero when I'm not? I'm a woman who is abandoning her child. Do you know how fucked up it is to have you hold me up as a saint?"

"I don't see it like that, Rachel," I say solemnly. "You could have terminated the pregnancy and never even told me about it. You could have terminated the pregnancy after you told me about it. No, you're not a saint, and I personally like the sinful side of you, but you are a good, decent human being. I find no fault with you if you don't want to be a mom. Plenty of women out there don't want to be—plenty of women who selflessly give their child up to a loving family—and anyone who thinks that's wrong is just living in the dark ages."

She doesn't respond, just lets her gaze drop to my chest while she nibbles on her lower lip.

"But Rachel," I say softly, and she looks slowly back up to me. "I don't believe for a second you don't want anything to do with the baby."

She doesn't agree with me, but she doesn't deny it either. Instead, she presses her hand to my chest. It touches me deeper than just her skin on mine. It's a hesitant plea almost. "What did you tell them about me?"

"Just the basics. That this wasn't a good time in your life. That you're at the height of your career, and you're amazing at what you do."

"Do they know that you and I are..."

"Fucking?" I ask with a grin.

"In a monogamous, sexual relationship," she counters with a glare.

"Ahh, you admit this is a relationship then?" I tease, my hand now going to her lower back to pull her in closer to me. "Yes... I told them that you and I were... well, together. For now."

"Until after the baby is born," she says. I hate that it makes me feel good, but I do like how she sounds glum about the notion.

I need to lighten the mood a little, because Rachel doesn't need to be stuck too deep into her thoughts. She's on the right path to figuring this out for herself. I'm confident she'll get there.

So I say, "They did have a concern."

"What's that?" she asks, her body stiffening in my arms.

"They're a little worried about the age difference," I say as seriously as I can. "My dad in particular... worried that a woman nine years older can't keep up with me."

Rachel just stares at me, uncomprehending such a thing.

"They figure at your age, your stamina probably isn't

what it used to—"

Her fingers give a hard, twisting pinch to my nipple, which causes me to yelp like a girl.

"You're an asshole," she mutters, and I laugh that she's so easily goaded. But then I'm not laughing when her mouth goes to my chest and her tongue eases the sting. My cock awakens and stirs restlessly against my leg.

"If you don't stop," I warn gruffly as my hand now moves up to cup the back of her head, holding her in place. "I'm going to fuck you again."

She licks around my nipple.

Presses a soft kiss there.

Lifting her head, she looks at me with a fire stoked back up in her eyes. "Yes. You *are* going to fuck me again."

CHAPTER 20

Rachel

ESTELLE AND GEORGE—or Geo as he likes to be called—are nothing and everything like I expected.

I knew because Bodie is a good, decent, and loyal man that his parents would be near about the same. I expected them to be kind, gracious, and down to earth. I expected them to be simple, but not in a bad way. Simple in that they derive their pleasures in life from simple things, mostly of which would be family.

What I didn't expect was how warm they would be to me. Maybe because Estelle is a farmer's wife and is used to taking care of people, she immediately cocooned me in a warm hug and proceeded to give me affirmation over the rough choices I've had to make. Maybe because Geo is a hardworking man with drive and dedication, he spent a lot of time asking me about what I do for Jameson, completely impressed that a woman can hang with the men.

They made me feel secure in where I stood at this

point in my life.

They made me realize it's okay to be a crazy mess of a woman who really doesn't know what she wants anymore. In no uncertain terms, they told me exactly what Bodie's been telling me... that it's okay to have doubts and fears, but that they were confident my heart would lead me to the right decision.

All of this occurred within just hours of meeting them. Bodie invited me to dinner with them, and I reluctantly agreed. I had to do it because Bodie told me his mom was going to come here as I got closer to the birth. She wanted to be on hand to help Bodie with the baby, so I needed to get to know her.

By the end of dinner, I honestly felt like I'd made two new friends in Estelle and Geo Wright. Bodie just smiled at me in a knowing way, confident as he always was that his parents would make me feel at ease with everything.

It's why I'm strolling arm and arm with Estelle along the midway, stopping periodically to watch Bodie and his dad participate in some game to win one of us a stuffed animal. Bodie invited me to go with his parents to the Boulder City Damboree to celebrate the Fourth of July. It started with a huge pancake breakfast this morning, which tasted especially delicious, so I had extra since I was eating for two. We then strolled through shops, listened to live music, and generally basked in the carnival-like atmosphere the town creates to celebrate

Independence Day. Tonight, there will be more music, and I'm told the best fireworks show in the entire Las Vegas valley.

"Let's try this one," Bodie says with the excitement of a five-year-old, giving his dad a slight punch to his shoulder. It's a classic 'pop a balloon with a dart' game, and Bodie is eyeballing a massive purple panda bear that is as big as I am.

Bodie and Geo pull their wallets out while Estelle and I stand back from them a bit, watching them try to win the big prize.

"Rachel," Estelle says softly, and it's a tone that has me cringing a bit. While we've had a general group discussion on the dynamics of what's going on with Bodie, the baby, and me, it's not gotten overly personal. Estelle's tone tells me it's about to. I turn to her, a placid look on my face. "I know you and Bodie have probably had some really deep talks about all of this, but I just wanted to offer my ear to you. I'm a mother and a woman, and I'm not sure if you've got girlfriends or family to support you, but I'm here if you need to talk. Even after I go back to Nebraska, you can call anytime."

A knot of emotion swells in my chest, more than honor or gratitude at her offer. It's almost like I fall a little bit in love with Bodie's mom right there and then.

I've never been close to my parents, and not because they are bad people. On the contrary, they sacrificed their relationship with their only daughter by letting me pursue my Olympic dreams. That meant I often lived away from them. Jacksonville, Florida wasn't exactly the best place for a winter athlete to train. So, from the time I was twelve until I left the Olympics, I lived mostly with training foster families out West where snow was plentiful, or I lived in the dorms at the U.S. Olympic Training Center in Colorado Springs, Colorado.

My time with my family was limited but focused, usually centered around holidays. My parents fully supported my dreams. They attended as many of my competitions as they could, but by the time I was sixteen, I was competing around the world. It just wasn't practical with their busy medical practices.

Sadly, the bond between us is strong by blood but weak by missed opportunities. I haven't even told my parents that I'm pregnant, although I will. Maybe I'll even fly to Florida to visit them soon.

A sudden yearning for my mom hits me from nowhere. A desire deep within me to just sit with my mom on a couch, put my head on her shoulder, and spill all my secrets. I'm not sure why I want it now. It's not something I've ever really yearned for, but I'd give anything for some security and understanding now.

"Estelle," I say impulsively as I turn to look at her fully. "I'd actually like to talk to you about something."

"Anything, honey," she says warmly, taking my hand in hers. "Let's go grab something to drink and sit down."

I nod mutely, happy to be given this opportunity.

"Bodie... Geo," Estelle calls out. They turn to look at us, eyes almost glazed with the hunt for a big stuffed animal. "We're going to go back up to the pavilion to get something to drink. Kick our feet up and relax a bit."

Geo nods absently, turning back to the game booth to pick up a dart. But Bodie's eyes become focused on me intently for a moment, trying to discern if I'm okay. I give him a smile, and he relaxes.

Nodding, he says, "Okay. You two have fun. We'll catch up to you later."

Estelle chatters about little things on the way to the pavilion, a huge open tent with drinks, vending, and tables to sit at to get out of the hot sun. We purchase some bottled waters but rather than sit under the tent, we choose a park bench that fortuitously sits under some shade trees and is looking rather abandoned and private.

Estelle doesn't waste time. The minute we sit down and before I can even uncap my water bottle, she asks, "So what did you want to talk about?"

"Well," I begin slowly. "You said something back there that struck me. You offered up your ear as a woman, and it really hit me... I need a woman's perspective."

"That's generally a good idea when you're talking about pregnancy and motherhood," she says with a tinkling laugh.

I smile and bob my head in agreement. I'm almost shy when I admit, "I don't have any girlfriends. I've never had much time to develop friendships of any sort, and because I work in such a male-dominated field, there aren't many female coworkers I could even bond with. Like me, they're all into the action and career aspects and we're all so busy, we just don't hang that much together."

"What about your mom?" she asks.

My smile grows fond and nostalgic. "Yes. I actually could talk to her, I believe. We're not super close because I was practically raised in other people's homes or at training facilities, but yeah... she's my mom and she'd give me good advice. But, you're here and she's not, and I feel like you'd be honest with me."

"Lay it on me," she says, slinging her arm over the back of the bench to turn more fully toward me. Her brown eyes—same as Bodie's—are soft and welcoming to my needs.

"I'm not sure if Bodie told you or not, but I've been having some second thoughts about the baby. About being involved in its life."

Estelle doesn't even raise her eyebrows. "He hasn't told me that, but I would think it would be natural to have conflicting feelings and doubts about any decision that involved a baby."

I nod. "I wasn't prepared for this. I thought I was solid in my decision, and then...week before last, I started spotting. It scared me so bad that I had to reevaluate everything, because when that happened, I was not ready to let this baby go. And it's nothing but a little tiny thing that can't survive outside of me yet. And I'm thinking… if the bond is that strong now, what the hell is going to happen to me when the baby is born? What will I feel when you and Bodie get on that plane and take the baby to Nebraska?"

Estelle doesn't respond right away, her expression thoughtful. She leans toward me, and her tone is strong and assured. "I know my son, and I am quite positive he's not pushing you one way or another. He's always content to let people make their own way. But I'm not going to be like that, because I am a mother and I know exactly what you are going to feel when we leave for Nebraska. Rachel… you're going to be crushed. You're going to be immersed in pain. You're going to drown in regret. You're going to hate yourself for missing out on all the wonderful and glorious things that happen with a newborn on a daily basis. Even if you change your mind a week after the baby is born, you're never going to forgive yourself for missing out on just a short seven days."

I lean back from Estelle, almost as if I want to escape her sharp words. They weren't said unkindly, but said so emphatically I can't help but believe her.

"What if I'm no good at it, though?" I ask on a whispered plea for her to tell me some truth that will make me feel more confident about everything.

She crushes me further by giving me the toughest of

love. "You might be bad at it at first. All new mothers have to learn their way. It's hard, and you're going to be an emotional mess through it all."

"You do know you should be trying to convince me to stay involved, right?" I say dryly.

Tilting her head back, Estelle gives a laugh. "Oh, honey... I'm not telling you anything you don't already know. You have everything you need to make your decision, and you don't strike me as the type of woman who is afraid of a challenge."

"I'm not," I say a bit too proudly, because now I'm feeling a little foolish for exposing my fears.

"Then what's the problem?" she asks bluntly.

So bluntly, it pierces my defenses like an arrow slicing through thin air. I blurt out another worry, and then I'm immediately ashamed. "Your son."

This time, Estelle does blink, but she quickly pulls a mask in place that reflects open curiosity and no condemnation. She silently waits for me to explain.

"He complicates things," I mutter, feeling horrible to even say that. My eyes drop down to my lap.

"Aha," she says in a knowing, enlightened way. "You have feelings for Bodie."

My head raises slowly, my eyes even slower, but I finally look at his mom. "Yeah... and you have to understand, I've never had feelings like this before. My entire life I've only been responsible for me. I've only answered to myself. And it's one thing for me to commit to a child… there's something biological and primal at work there. But with Bodie? I'm more scared of that than I am of being a mother."

Estelle's eyes grow softly luminescent, and her happiness that there's someone who cares for her son is obvious. She reaches out and takes my hand. "That I can't help you with. I've only ever loved Geo, so I don't know much about the game of finding love. Geo was always right there since ninth grade. But I can tell you that when you do find love—true love—it's about the most wonderful thing in the world."

"So they say," I murmur, appreciating that Estelle is pushing the beauty of love rather than the hard work and sacrifice. God knows I've got enough of that facing me with a baby on the way.

"Just let it be," Estelle suggests, and it sounds like sage advice because it's the easiest thing for me right now. "Just wait and see what happens. If it's meant to be, it will be."

Estelle drops my hand and nods at something over my shoulder. I don't bother looking when she says, "Our menfolk are coming this way, but one last piece of advice, okay?"

I nod quickly.

"Keep your heart open, Rachel. I suspect you're the type of person who has become so accustomed to being alone that you don't know how to share it. But if you just keep it open, even a little, to let someone else in, I think you'll find that the benefits far outweigh the fears."

I don't even have time to assure her I'll take her advice, because a massive purple and white panda bear is dropped from above into my lap. It's so huge my arms can't even fit all the way around it. I tip my head way back and see Bodie hovering over me.

"Finally got that damn bear," he says with a blinding grin.

"How much money did it cost you?" I ask.

"Only seventy-two dollars," he says with a laugh. "So, you better enjoy it."

I don't say it out loud, but I think to myself, *This would look awesome in the baby's nursery.*

I also wonder what the nursery would look like. Would we decorate it with cliché or our own personal style?

All questions that lead me to believe that what I thought I wanted when I first found out I was pregnant is not what I want at all right now.

CHAPTER 21

Bodie

I'VE SEEN SOME shit in my time as a SEAL and working at Jameson. Bullet wounds, broken bones, guts spilling out. I once saw a man jump off a three-story building and land on his head. It popped like a grape, and brains splattered all over.

Blood and gore never bothered me, but when the doctor pulls a fucking eight-inch-long needle out of its protective wrap, knowing he's going to stick that in Rachel's stomach, my knees go a little weak.

I'm standing by the examination table at her side, and my hand blindly reaches out to hers. She gives me a comforting squeeze, and I realize it's the first time since Rachel and I started on this journey that she's the one giving me support.

The thought is almost laughable, but I'm afraid if I open my mouth, I'll puke.

Rachel just lays there like this is nothing. She even has her other hand propped under her head to raise it, so she can watch what's going on.

Dr. Anchors has already run the ultrasound wand over her lower belly and located the baby's position. He did that while the local anesthetic he gave her was working its mojo. Now he gets all his implements ready, which is basically just a big fucking needle he's going to stick in my woman.

The doctor has laid a blue sterile paper over Rachel's lap, which is where he puts the needle. I watch uneasily as he rubs a gauze soaked with a reddish-brown antiseptic all over her belly. She's at fifteen weeks now and according to the internet, the baby is as big as a navel orange. I read that last night after Rachel went to sleep. It seems awful big, which means there's not a lot of room in there for the doctor to make a mistake.

Just thinking about that again causes my anxiety to flare. I want to scoop Rachel off the table and run.

I get another squeeze of her hand in mine, and my gaze travels to meet hers. She's staring at me knowingly, but she doesn't make a big deal out of my fears. I give her hand a squeeze back, but that's not enough. Bending over, I put my lips to her forehead and whisper, "Brave girl."

"Okay," Dr. Anchors says. I pull back from Rachel to watch. I don't want to, but I'm going to because it's the least I can do. "Let's get started."

A nurse moves in close with the top of the syringe that will draw the fluid out. It's oddly shaped—a rectangular-looking unit with a pull lever and cylindrical container in the middle for the fluid. Dr. Anchors puts the ultrasound wand back to Rachel's belly and quickly locates the baby. My breath catches much as it did the first time, and I sneak a quick peek at Rachel. She's staring at the ultrasound screen with large eyes full of wonder.

Dr. Anchors holds the wand in place and carefully takes the needle in his other hand. He deftly pierces her abdomen, pushing it down through her uterine wall. My head swims for a moment, but then I blink it away. The nurse moves in, attaches the thing she's holding in her hand to the cap on the needle, and pulls the lever. The cylindrical container fills with a golden yellow liquid. She pulls on it slowly but steadily, and I get a little dizzy again at the amount of fluid coming out.

My eyes cut to the screen and I have to swallow hard when I see the needle hovering so very close to the baby. My hand reflexively bears down on Rachel, but I don't care at this point. I assume she'll pay me back during childbirth.

When the tube is filled, the nurse disconnects from the needle, and then Dr. Anchors is pulling it free. He moves the wand a little, checks the baby again, and then pronounces, "All done."

"That wasn't so bad," Rachel says lightly.

Dr. Anchors chuckles. "I find that the women usually have an easier time than the men with that procedure."

"Not this man," I say in a deep, confident voice with my chest puffed out slightly. Thank God, the nausea has passed.

"While most of the results will take a few weeks, we'll have the gender back in a few days," Dr. Anchors says as he pulls off his gloves. A nurse dries Rachel from the antiseptic that had dripped down her sides, and when she's done, I help her sit up on the table.

"It's a boy," Rachel says as she comes up to the sitting position.

"Oh, yeah?" Dr. Anchors says with interest. He pushes up from the stool and goes to the sink to wash his hands. "I believe Bodie declared it was a girl on the last visit."

"It's definitely a boy," she says confidently. "I just know it."

"You didn't tell me that," I say somewhat accusingly. Many of our discussions focus around the baby and the pregnancy, and my little proclamation about it being a girl was just a joke. I have no clue whatsoever.

"I didn't know it until just a little bit ago, when we saw him on the screen. And then I just knew."

"Huh," I say in contemplation. She's so confident about it, I sort of believe her. I could totally handle a son. But then a thought hits me. "I've got a weird request, though."

"What's that?" Rachel asks.

"I don't want to know the sex just yet." Rachel

doesn't even look surprised. In fact, she has sort of a knowing smirk on her face. "I mean... I don't want to find out by Dr. Anchors calling us in two days. It's kind of—"

"Anticlimactic?" Dr. Anchors suggests.

"Not traditional," I suggest instead as I turn to the doctor. "It's just... I sort of imagined it would be via an ultrasound and Rachel and I would be looking at the screen, not able to even understand what we're looking at, and then you will point at a spot on the screen and say something like, 'Look... it's a penis.' And then I'll yell 'yee-haw,' and Rachel will be like, 'I told you so,' and—"

Rachel starts laughing and claps me on the shoulder. "Fine. Let's not find out the gender until the next visit with an ultrasound."

Dr. Anchors chuckles as he dries his hands. "I'll note in the file not to call you with results, and believe it or not, you're not the first parents who have requested to find out via ultrasound."

"It's a plan," Rachel says with a smile.

Dr. Anchors reaches his hand out, shakes Rachel's, and then mine. He and the nurse clear out of the room, and Rachel hops off the table.

I reach over to a chair in the corner and pick up her clothes. As I hand them to her, I ask, "How did that really feel?"

As Rachel shrugs on her jeans, she says, "It felt weird.

The needle burned at first, then I felt a little crampy when they started taking the fluid out."

She stands up straight to button and zip her jeans. "It hurt a hell of a lot more getting shot."

"I thought I was going to pass out there for a moment," I admit sheepishly. "I don't know how you were so calm."

I expect Rachel to laugh at me. Poke at me a little. Tease me good and proper.

Instead, she steps into me and wraps her arms around my waist. "Thank you for being by my side. That's why it didn't bother me that much."

Jesus. Sometimes, the things this woman says make me want to believe in all kinds of potential for our future.

Makes me think we could have something amazing if Rachel were to ever let loose and open herself up.

When she pulls back from me, she moves over to the chair to put her socks and tennis shoes on. I check my watch, mentally calculating the things I need to do tonight. I'm leaving tomorrow for Egypt. It's an intelligence-gathering mission we're subcontracting on with a special forces group and the CIA. We don't know what the objective is yet, but we'll be filled in during transport out of Washington.

I hate to leave Rachel, not only because I'm going to miss her, but also because I worry about her. Everything has been fine since the spotting a few weeks ago, and our sex life is as active as ever. Rachel has even appeared more settled since my parents' visit last week, and I like the routine we're in.

I'm still staying at Rachel's each night. She's not asked me to leave, and I've not offered. I merely go to my house every few days to do laundry and check my mail.

As Rachel ties her last lace, I ask, "Mind if we do takeout or something easy tonight? I've got a ton of stuff to do to get ready for the trip."

"I want to keep the baby," Rachel blurts as she stands up. If she had a feather in her hand, she could have knocked me over with it.

Her cheeks pinken with embarrassment. "I didn't mean to just say it like that. But I couldn't quite figure out how to bring it up."

My shocked senses are having a hard time catching up to what she's saying. "When did you decide this?"

She gives a tiny shrug, crossing her arms protectively over her belly. "If I'm honest, that day I was spotting. I just think it took this long for me to admit it out loud."

"This is huge," I murmur as I step into her. I pull her arms away from her torso, and then lay my hand over the spot where our little orange is hibernating. "Are you sure?"

She nods effusively, but her voice is still wary. "Will you stay here if I do this? Don't go to Nebraska. I'd really like to stay on at Jameson, and this means you could as well. But I don't know how set you are about going back home now. I mean... your parents are awesome times ten, so why wouldn't you want to go there?"

I shake my head. "I'd rather stay at Jameson. Here in Vegas. With you."

Special emphasis in my head on the "with you," but I don't push that just yet. It's enough that Rachel wants to raise the baby with me.

It's a decision I knew she'd get right in the long run.

"When you get back from this trip to Egypt, we'll have the ultrasound where we find out the baby's gender. I thought we could maybe decide how to decorate the nursery then. Maybe go out shopping for some things."

I have to control myself.

Because in this moment, I want to let out a whooping holler, pick Rachel up, and spin her around. She's grabbed onto this baby thing by the horns, and I couldn't be happier. All the things I thought I'd have to do on my own now can be done with a partner beside me.

"Sure," I say casually. "That would be a lot of fun. And a name. We'd be able to start talking about a name."

"I'm partial to Keegan," she says.

"And I'm not," I say without any hesitation.

"Asher?"

"Nope."

"Evan?"

"Fuck no."

"Logan?"

"Just shoot me now," I groan in mock misery, and then I grin at her. "Okay, maybe Logan isn't so bad. But you know, it could be a girl."

"It's a boy," she says, and her confidence in the prediction has not weakened in the slightest.

"Come on." I put my arm around her and turn her toward the door. "Let's go figure out something for dinner, let me start some laundry so I can get packed, and then we can argue about it while we eat."

"Deal," she says with a laugh. As we walk out of the doctor's office, I realize I'm not quite sure I've ever been this happy.

Yes, a lot of it has to do with the fact I can stop worrying about Rachel and how a bad decision could have ruined her. I can also rejoice in the fact I can stay on at Jameson.

But mostly, I'm happy that things will continue between Rachel and me. I sure as hell don't want to give her up, and I'm hopeful she's feeling the same.

That's a discussion for another time.

For now, I'll just be happy.

CHAPTER 22

Rachel

I CLOSE THE thin manila folder and slide it in my shoulder satchel. I've got the company credit card and thirty minutes to get to the airport to catch my flight.

Kynan approached me yesterday about taking this trip on his behalf. He was slated to fly to Chicago to scope out a venue Jameson would be providing security for. It was a fundraising gala that would see Hollywood's biggest stars along with a good chunk of prominent politicians. Kynan hates shit like this, so I wasn't surprised he asked.

Wasn't surprised I accepted, even though I hate shit like this, too.

But Bodie's been gone for six days. He's not due back for at least another week, and I'm bored and lonely. This will keep my mind busy for a few days and help the time to pass.

God, I can't believe how much I miss him. Never even considered I would, since we've not been apart much since I got pregnant. There's no doubt we're in a relationship now, but I'm just not sure what that means.

If I'd been asked six days ago, I would have said it only meant that we were sort of living together, having amazing sex, and would soon be raising a kid together. Very simple.

But Bodie left and within one day, I was battling an empty, haunted feeling inside of me. The house was too quiet. My meals were too bland. Books I read were too boring, and the orgasms I gave myself were lackluster.

It's been incredibly frustrating, but enlightening at the same time.

My feelings for Bodie clearly have more depth than I ever would have imagined. I even wonder if this could be the start of love for me.

"Rachel…" Kynan's voice comes from the doorway of the spare office I'd been using today at Jameson's headquarters.

I turn to face him. "What's up?"

"Need you to come down to my office," he says, and my heart sinks over the tone of his voice. It's flat and bleak, causing chills of apprehension to race up my spine.

I scramble after him, practically jogging to catch up, and follow him to his office. Jerico is sitting in one of the chairs, along with a man I don't recognize in a dark suit and tightly cropped hair.

CIA, I'd guess.

"What's going on?" My voice trembles with fear

because I know there's only one reason they would call me into a meeting with a spook, and that's because Bodie is out on a mission right now in conjunction with them.

"Renegade 1 came under fire night before last," Kynan says gravely. "They had to split up. Most of them made it back to the rendezvous point."

"But not Bodie," I manage to conclude in a hoarse voice. My hand goes to my stomach, perhaps protecting Bodie's child from the worst possible news.

"Nor Cage," Kynan adds, and my stomach flips at the thought of Bodie and his best friend being on the run from monsters in the dark.

"The Navy has a SEAL team on the ground now searching," the CIA dude says. At least I think he's CIA, but I really don't give a fuck. Just as long as he gets Bodie and Cage out of there.

"I'm sending Sal in your place to Chicago," Kynan says, and I can do nothing but nod my agreement. I'm not leaving Jameson's offices until Bodie's home safe and sound.

"Rachel... they're in deep," he says, and I can tell by the hint of pessimism in his voice that he's setting me up for the possibility of failure. "In a mountainous region just north of Adana. Really deep. Their locator signals are on and transmitting, but it could be tricky getting them out."

I knew this trip was going to be risky. Gathering intelligence on our enemies always is. More and more, the U.S. government has been contracting out its need for resources in the form of private companies like ours to provide the intelligence they need.

"When will we know something?" I ask, refusing to even consider Kynan's implied suggestion that they may not be recoverable.

"Hopefully soon," the spook says evasively, and I want to strangle him.

"You should go home," Kynan suggests softly. "I'll keep you updated."

"I'm not leaving until I know Bodie is safe," I growl, and he just inclines his head in understanding. Jerico watches me thoughtfully, but doesn't say a word.

"She's not cleared—" the CIA douche starts to say, but Kynan glares at him.

"She's staying. Get her clearance if you need to, but she's not going anywhere."

The man steps out of Kynan's office, putting his phone up to his ear to make a call. Kynan walks back around his desk, and sits down with a heavy sigh. Jerico stands up from his chair and pats the back. "Come sit down, Rachel. It's going to be a long day."

I don't think to argue with Jerico. Besides, my legs are so rubbery from fear I'm afraid I might just pitch over onto the carpet. I take the chair, and Jerico moves to the window to stare out of it.

I'm not surprised he's here. He's got no stake in the company, but he's Kynan's best friend. I know the safety of all the people here are still of great importance to him. Of course he'd be here.

I also suspect Jerico is here because he has important contacts in the government. If he suspects that not every available resource is being used to get our guys back, he's going to start making calls to the top brass.

Pulling my phone out, I flip to my photos. I have pathetically few, and hardly any of people. I might take a photo of a pretty sunset or an interesting flower, but for the most part, I don't preserve memories except within my head.

But the very last photo on my camera roll, taken the night Bodie was packing for this trip, is perhaps my favorite in the world.

It's of Bodie and me together. We were laying naked in bed, having just had utterly amazing sex, and he started teasing me.

"You're going to miss me when I'm gone, aren't you, Hart?" he'd asked as he rolled on his side to look at me.

"Not in the slightest," I said airily. "I'm tired of you hogging all the covers at night anyway."

"You're so going to miss me," he said tauntingly. "Probably will sit by the window, shedding some tears, waiting anxiously for my truck to pull back in the driveway. Fuck, you'll probably have a million yellow ribbons tied around every tree in the neighborhood."

I'd scoffed and rolled my eyes. "Totally delusional, Wright."

He winked and laughed.

I rolled away from him, snagged my phone off the bedside table, and turned on the camera app. Holding it up, I snapped a quick picture of his face. "There. I got your face right here so I won't be missing you at all."

Bodie was the one who rolled his eyes. He reached a long arm out, grabbed his own phone, and proclaimed, "That's not a proper picture."

Before I knew what he was doing, he had me dragged over onto his body, my face resting next to his. He held the camera out and said, "Smile."

I'd had to tilt my head and crane my neck a little to look, but there we were. Bodie and me with our faces right beside each other on his camera, which was in selfie mode. He'd been grinning like a lunatic.

I'd been mesmerized by the sight.

Me and Bodie together.

He looked so happy.

I looked dazzled.

He snapped the photo and then immediately texted it to me. I pretended it didn't mean anything, and it was soon forgotten because Bodie put his hands and mouth on me and well, who could think at that point?

But after he left the next day… when I first realized that I did miss him, I'd pulled that photo up. Not the one of just Bodie I'd taken, but the one Bodie had texted to me.

I'd saved it in my favorites.

It was the only photo in my favorites.

I become vaguely aware of Jerico, Kynan, and the CIA guy talking as they stand around Kynan's desk, looking at some maps that had been rolled out.

I catch words like "eventuality," "extraction point," and "any force necessary".

Kynan's voice lowers, but I can still hear them talking about the possibility of body retrieval.

My eyes focus in on the photo of Bodie and me. I stare at it so hard my eyes burn and his face starts to blur around the edges.

Pain pierces me right in the center of my chest, so exquisite that my breath is knocked out of me and bile rises in my throat. I lurch up from the chair, and all of their heads snap my way.

"Rachel?" Jerico asks with concern in his voice.

"Need to use the restroom," I rasp, it actually hurting to get the words out. I turn away from them and hurry from the room, grasping my phone so hard in my hand that my bones ache.

I scurry into the women's restroom and press my back against the door when it closes. My breaths are coming out in sharp pants, and the pain in my chest intensifies to the point I worry I might be having a heart attack.

But I know that's not true.

I'm feeling the searing pain of grief, believing I've already lost Bodie before I could even tell him that I was so glad I found him. It hurts worse than anything I could have ever imagined. A million times more intense than when I miscarried all those years ago. The pain of a thousand bullets ripping through me.

"Oh, God," I groan as I slide down the door until my ass hits the floor. I bring my knees up and press my forehead to them, acutely aware that I'm in so much pain I can't even cry.

A racking, dry sob bursts out of me. An image of me walking our son to Bodie's grave flits through my mind. How can I tell him all about his daddy when I didn't get enough time with him myself to know all there was to know? I've only got a few months of memories to share, and now a lifetime to regret everything.

Tears finally sting at my eyes, hot and burning. Another stab of pain in my chest... a gurgling sob. I wrap my arms around my stomach—around our baby—and I just let myself grieve.

I open up and take the pain.

Breathe through it the way I might when I go into labor.

I'm startled when the bathroom door nudges at my back, but it immediately stops when it meets resistance.

"Rachel?" It's Kynan on the other side.

I scramble to my feet, wiping my face with my hands to dry the tears. After I open the door, I look at him expectantly.

"Just got an update. They've been located in a small

temporary camp. It's not well defended."

"Are they okay?" I ask as I walk out of the bathroom.

"They haven't made visual contact. It's some abandoned buildings with only four men who patrol around the area. We're guessing that's where they're holding Cage and Bodie."

"Or where they're holding their clothing, which have the trackers sewn into the lining?" I point out fearfully.

"Infrared confirms there are two people inside the building the signal is coming from," he returns in a low voice. "It's them."

"Okay," I say as I breathe out, feeling the pain in my chest lessen minutely. Infrared means there's body heat, which means they're alive.

"We'll know soon," Kynan says. He turns back toward his office. "It's only about 11:30 PM there now. The SEALs are going to hit just before dawn."

Just a handful of hours that I have left to hope Bodie is alive and safe in that building, and this rescue goes off without any bloodshed on our part. In a handful of hours, I'll know if that torturous grief I'd been experiencing just moments ago in the bathroom was just a preview of what's to come if Bodie doesn't make it out of there.

CHAPTER 23

Bodie

MY EYES FLUTTER open, and I can't help the groan of pain that slices through the center of my brain as the light filters in. I snap them shut again, the blessed dark providing some relief.

"Bodie?" a voice calls. It sounds hollow, like it's at the end of a long tunnel. For a moment, I think maybe it's God calling me to join him in the light or something, but fuck that… I'm not ready.

Plus, that light hurts like hell.

"I think he's waking up," the voice says.

Another one says, "I'll get Kynan."

Kynan?

Kynan's here?

I struggle out of the black, open my eyes to barely slits so it turns gray. Two figures are hovering over me.

Pain throbs in my head, causing me to groan. It feels heavy, and I can't lift it. I try to lift my hand to rub against the ache, but it won't move.

"Don't move that arm, buddy," the first voice says, and I recognize it now.

Jerico Jameson.

I push against the pain and open my eyes. The two figures go from blurry to just fuzzy. Jerico is to my left and Kynan is to my right.

"About time you fucking woke up, slacker," Kynan says with a grin. I have no clue what's going on, but I can hear the relief in his voice. I try to smile, but fuck... even that hurts, so I don't make it past a grimace.

"What happened to me?" I say, but my words are slurred as they try to make their way past a thick tongue that feels like it's glued to the top of my mouth.

"Get him some of that water," Jerico says. The next thing I know, there's a straw pushing in my mouth. "Just a few sips."

I try to pull hard because I'm so damn thirsty, but I get no more than a few drops down my throat before the straw is pulled away.

"Where am I?" I ask as my eyes sluggishly move around what is clearly a hospital room.

"You're at University Medical Center," Kynan says. "They had to put some pins in your elbow. You smashed it good on a rock or something."

I lift my head to look at my arm, but the resulting pain makes me squeeze my eyes shut for the sweet dark again.

"Yeah, don't try to do that either. You had a pretty

bad head wound. I'm guessing another rock—"

"Rifle butt," I mutter when it starts to come back to me. I let my eyes open again. "Cage and I slid down a really long rocky embankment trying to take cover. I took a bad tumble; hit my elbow on a rock. Later... when they found us, I took a hit to the back of the head when I tried resist. Cage was—"

I stop a moment, horror filling me. My entire body lurches upward despite the pain and immobility. "Cage... what happened to him?"

"Easy," Jerico says with a hand to my shoulder to ease me back down. "Cage is fine."

"He was shot—"

"And he was rescued right along with you. He's recovering on the next floor up. He got out of surgery about the same time you did. He's going to be completely fine."

I sag in relief. He'd taken a bullet to his calf. While I'd managed to dress it sufficiently to stop the bleeding, I knew that every hour that went by without some real medical help might mean he could lose it.

"And everyone else?" I ask. All I remember is being ambushed in the middle of the night while we were set up on a short perimeter to gather photos and take notes of our observations to report back. It was on a small town at the base of the Tahtali mountains where a small suspected ISIS cell was developing. We were getting details on the number of people in general broken down by men, women, and children, as well as an estimate on the weaponry.

"Everyone is fine. The rest of the team made it out, and we sent in a SEAL team to get you and Cage."

I give a slight nod and learn very quickly it's better to keep still. "How long do I have to stay in here?"

"I'm not sure," Jerico answers. "Your head is apparently hard as hell; that's all checked out. Your elbow was pretty bad, so they had to put some hardware in to piece it back together."

I glance down. My arm is bent at the elbow in a natural forty-five-degree angle, and splinted and wrapped from wrist to shoulder. It's absolutely immobile.

That's going to make it a little difficult to fuck Rachel properly, but I'm sure—

I lurch off the bed again. "Where's Rachel?"

"Jesus, you're a mess," Jerico mutters as he gently pushes me back down. When my head settles onto the pillow, which feels about as hard as the rifle butt, Jerico steps to the side. Rachel is sitting across the room in a chair.

She sits straight, her hands held together in her lap, legs pressed together. She just stares at me, and I can't read a thing on her face.

She finally stands from the chair, wiping her hands on the denim covering her thighs, and it seems her movements are hesitant. Her face is impassively blank.

"Let's go get some coffee," Jerico suggests to Kynan,

but I don't bother looking at either of them.

I only have eyes for Rachel. I'd imagined her face... her body... our baby... practically every minute of every hour we were held prisoner. I'd like to be the hero and have some glamorous story about how Cage and I were tortured for information, but they actually dumped us in an abandoned house and left us there. I was confident we were being held for some higher-ups within ISIS to question us, but thankfully we were rescued before then.

So, I thought of her incessantly. Sadly, I had no chance to dream about her because sleep was impossible with a crushed elbow and what felt like my brains leaking out of the back of my head.

When Rachel makes it to the side of my bed—the side with the busted elbow—I can see the dark circles under her eyes and the grim set to her lips. I want to reach my hand out to touch her.

To comfort her.

But I can't.

Her eyes roam all over my face. I have no clue what it looks like, but I try to put on a cheerful look despite how crappy I feel. None of that matters now that I'm back home.

"You scared a lot of people back home," she says quietly, her hands gripping the bed rail so hard her knuckles are white.

"Are you okay?" I ask, my eyes drifting to her belly.

"Yeah," she says in a raspy, dull voice. "Me and the

baby are fine."

"You don't sound fine," I say flatly. I sort of imagined she'd be overjoyed to see me alive and well.

"I thought you had died." I didn't think it was possible, but her voice is flatter than mine.

"But I didn't," I reply in a singsong voice, trying to make her smile.

It doesn't work. Her expression darkens, and her blue eyes turn almost gray with pain.

"Hey," I say softly, my busted arm involuntarily trying to move to her, but it's held in place. I sigh with frustration, and use my voice only. "It's okay. I'm fine."

"I can see that," she murmurs. She even attempts a half-hearted smile, but it doesn't obliterate the gray in her eyes.

"I heard my boy was awake." It's my mom's voice coming through the door. Rachel turns and looks over her shoulder.

My mom walks in followed by my dad, who is carrying a cardboard tray with three large Styrofoam cups with lids.

Rachel backs away from the bed so my mom can come in. She smiles down at me the way I wanted Rachel to, eyes brimming with happy tears. Her hand comes to my face. "You had me so scared, Bodie Allen Wright."

"Uh-oh," I say jokingly. "Used my middle name and everything. I must be in trouble."

My eyes cut to Rachel. My dad hands her a cup—

tea, I imagine—setting the tray with the other two still entrenched on a rolling bedside table. He steps up beside my mom, completely blocking my view of Rachel.

Dropping her hand from my face, my mom holds onto the rail with both hands and leans over me. Her eyes shimmer with love and relief. "I know you probably don't want to hear this, but I'm so damn happy you're going to be coming to Nebraska after the baby is born. Then I can stop worrying about you getting killed."

I chuckle but that hurts my head, so I cut it off sharply. "Sorry to disappoint you, Mom, but I'm going to be staying. Rachel wants to keep the baby... raise it with me. So I'm staying here, and we'll both continue at Jameson. Didn't she tell you?"

My parents have been here long enough—given they were all sitting in my room waiting for me to wake up—that I assumed the subject would come up. I didn't get a chance to tell them before I left last week, figuring I'd call them with the news when I got back.

I lean slightly to the left to try to see around my mom to Rachel, intent on perhaps giving her a reproachful look for not telling my mom. She probably felt it wasn't her place, though, so I decide just a smile will be good enough.

Except I don't see Rachel.

I try to lean further, and my mom gets the picture. She steps back, and she and my father both turn to Rachel.

Except... Rachel is just gone.

Silently ghosting out without a word.

"She probably stepped out to give us some privacy," my mom says in a cheery voice. "Although why she would do that is beyond me. We're almost family, you know."

My mother's eyes are on me expectantly, wanting me to be happy just to be alive the way she is. I'm feeling all kinds of dark inside, though, because I know damn well Rachel didn't step out just to give us privacy.

She ran away from me.

"Bodie?" my mom says gently, calling my attention to her rather than the empty doorway my eyes had drifted to.

I pull a smile on my face, turning to look at my mom. "Yeah... I'm sure she'll be back soon. Now, tell me the details that Kynan and Jerico left out. I don't even know what day it is."

My mom starts to chatter. She tells me we had been rescued day before last and somehow ferreted out to a U.S. Naval ship on maneuvers close by. I vaguely remember this, but I also remember them giving me painkillers, so I was floating high. After talking to the Navy doctors on the ship who felt we were well stabilized, Kynan made a judgment call to have us flown via a C17 medical flight to March Air Force Reserve Base in California. From there, we took a private medical flight home to Vegas, making it back in thirty-two hours from the time of our rescue. Surgeons were on standby and waiting when we arrived.

I continue to get the low down on my medical condition. Listening half-heartedly, I know there's not a damn thing I can do to change circumstances.

A doctor comes in and checks me over. He says if I do well overnight, I can go home tomorrow.

A nursing assistant comes later and takes my vitals.

Lunch arrives, and my mom has to help feed me because I'm still groggy and awkward with my busted arm.

A nurse brings pain meds, and I have no choice but to nap.

When I wake up, my parents are still there.

Rachel never returns.

CHAPTER 24

Rachel

I SIT IN the stiff plastic chair directly across from Bodie's bed. My ass went numb a long time ago, and I don't need to look at the clock to know I've been here for almost six hours. Bodie didn't even see me when the nurse came in around three AM to check his vitals. He woke up, but was groggy. I sat in the shadows in the corner of his room and just watched. By the time the nurse shot me a smile and walked out, he was out and snoring again.

I just watched him.

For hours.

Watched his chest rise, up and down. Slow and steady.

It was the most beautiful thing ever.

The room is starting to lighten with the approaching sunrise. I should take the opportunity while he's still sleeping to go down and get some hot tea and maybe a bagel. I'm going to need the fuel today since I've had almost zero sleep the last four days.

And yet, I can't seem to make myself leave. He could wake up, and I don't want him to see an empty room. I want him to see *me*.

Here for him.

My phone vibrates where it sits on my thigh. It's from Estelle. *Everything going okay?*

I quickly text back, *He's still sleeping. I'll let you know when he's awake.*

Estelle and Geo are staying at a hotel rather than at Bodie's house, which is out of the way. They left after Bodie had fallen asleep last night. Estelle had texted me as much. She was very much aware I had left without a word and not returned throughout the day. My message was clear to everyone, even though I wasn't trying to send one. I was just trying to process feelings, and I think she knows that. I wonder if she explained that to Bodie to reassure him.

I didn't come back to the hospital until almost midnight. Prior to that, I'd been sitting in my dark living room, alternately looking at the photo of Bodie and me and staring at the opposite wall that was barely lit by moonlight through the window.

My eyes carefully roam over Bodie as he sleeps. It might be the millionth time I've done it since I came back to the hospital. I can't see it, but I know there is a gauze bandage on the back of his head covering some staples. Throughout the night, he's been shifting around, clearly uncomfortable from the elbow injury. He would grimace in his sleep. Sometimes, he'd mutter obscenities. Once, I even heard him say my name.

I wanted to run up to his bed, shake him awake, and tell him I was here. My name on his lips filled me with warmth—as if a sunbeam had been shining down upon me. Even in his drug-induced sleep, Bodie was thinking about me.

It felt almost as good as when Bodie first woke up in the hospital bed. There's just no word in the English language that can adequately describe the emotions I felt upon seeing his eyes open. It was the first time since this nightmare started that I felt true confidence he would be okay. Even though I had known for more than forty hours that Bodie was alive, safe, and would have a good recovery from his injuries, it never seemed real until he woke up.

Relief and joy was what I had expected to feel. But in those moments after his eyes fluttered open, all the pain and grief I had been feeling when Kynan first told me he was missing came flooding back. All I could do was stare down at him, wanting to hate him for making me love him, and wanting to hate Kynan for sending him into danger. Mostly I wanted to hate myself for falling so hard for him.

Of course, it was ludicrous to think those thoughts, and I know I was beyond irrational. All I could seem to focus on was that it was the very reason why it was better to be alone. It kept playing over and over that it was why I never bothered with relationships. They were too hard. The stakes were too high. The risk was too great. The pain was unbearable when it didn't work out.

I'm so ashamed of myself, but I couldn't stand to even look at him anymore. Bodie—true, honest, and wise-for-his-age Bodie—knew in that moment I was struggling. He tried to make light of his condition just to make me smile.

That smile broke me, and my shame burned brighter because I couldn't stand to be around him. I used Estelle and Geo's entrance into the room to make my escape, and it *was* an escape.

I was escaping the prison I'd let myself get trapped in, built on pain and fear. It was an escape back to a life I knew well, one without any responsibilities or ties that could hold me down.

God, I was so stupid to even feel that way, and I can only hope Bodie truly understands me.

A groan from the bed startles me, and my gaze sharpens on Bodie. His head rolls on the pillow, and his good arm subconsciously reaches across to scratch at the splint on the other. His face wrinkles with confusion as his fingers touch the wrapping, and then his eyes pop wide open.

Bodie lifts his head up and looks down at his arm. Understanding dawns through his grogginess, and his head starts to fall back as he sighs. But his eyes snag on me before his head hits the pillow, and he freezes. Bodie stares at me an inordinately long time, just blinking his eyes as if he cannot believe I'm sitting there.

"Rachel?" he says in a froggy voice.

"Morning," I tell him softly.

Bodie's head falls to the pillow and rolls to the right. He looks out the window at the dawn sky before turning back to me. "How long have you been here?"

"About six hours," I say.

"Just sitting there watching me?"

"Pretty much."

"That's kind of creepy, you know?" His lips are tipped up with his trademark humor, and I know I've already been forgiven for succumbing to my fears.

And God, he looks so beautiful even broken and beaten in a hospital bed.

I stand up from the chair and arch my back to stretch. After I place my cell phone on the seat I had just vacated, I walk to the side of Bodie's bed. I come to stand right by where his injured elbow is resting on a smaller pillow. I don't say anything for a few reasons. First, because it's hard for me to express my feelings, but mostly because I know Bodie will lead the conversation to where it needs to go in the most efficient way.

He'll make the important statements.

Ask the questions that need asked.

Tell me his conclusions.

"You ran," he says emphatically.

I nod. "I did."

"And now you've come back," he says in a voice as soft as velvet. "Is this to tell me goodbye?"

I shake my head, giving an apologetic smile. It's both tragic and sad that he's even having to ask me that question. "I came back because I was remiss yesterday in not telling you that I love you."

Bodie's body jumps almost imperceptibly, as if someone had given him a tiny pinch to his ass or something.

"You were remiss yesterday by not telling me that?" He looks at me with something in his eyes that I've never quite seen from him before. It's a measure of excitement mixed with tenderness. I see hopefulness and yearning there as well.

I lift my gaze and look out the window. The sky is pink and orange, and it makes me feel hopeful.

"When Kynan told me what happened," I say as I let my eyes wander back to his face. "Something happened to me that I've never felt in my entire life. It was a barrenness inside of me because I thought the worst... that you had died. The emptiness was so painful that my world turned gray. I know I'm not describing it right, Bodie, but it was the worst thing I've ever felt. It scared me so bad that hopelessness was all I could feel. I didn't know... that such emotions were possible. I didn't get it then, but I know now... what I was feeling was heartbreak and grief over losing you. And I was so mad,

Bodie. At you and Kynan and Jerico and the fucking people who captured you. At myself, most of all. Because I should have never let myself get involved with you."

"That explains why you didn't look like you were happy to see me yesterday," Bodie says dryly. I get by the smart-ass smirk on his face that he's teasing me.

I give a tiny laugh. "I didn't know whether to smack you or kiss you."

"You panicked instead and ran."

"I'm sorry," I say. I reach over the rail and place my hand in the middle of his chest. I don't want to take his hand for fear I'll somehow hurt the attached elbow.

"Don't," he says softly, bringing the hand on his good arm over to cover mine. He squeezes softly, then lifts my hand to his mouth. He brushes his lips on my fingertips, then returns my hand to his chest where he has me flatten my palm right over his heart. "You're here now telling me exactly what I want to hear. That's all that matters."

There's no condemnation—which I deserve—only understanding, and I'm not sure I could love him more than I do right now.

It hits me hard.

I love Bodie.

I even told him I loved him, and really didn't think twice. It wasn't hard. My words didn't falter. I spoke from the heart, and that's what came out of my mouth.

It might have taken me a bit of a shake up and a

moment of tremendous doubt in myself to get here, but goddamn it... I'm here now and I'm not leaving.

"I'd kill to know what you're thinking right now," Bodie says, breaking into my thoughts.

I give a hard shake of my head. "Nothing that you don't already know. I'm a chicken shit, and I had a minor freak out over the strength of my feelings."

"I've always known you're the type of person who will get to your best destination when you're damn good and ready. And Rachel... you panicked for a few hours last night. Not sure that's really something to worry about."

Leaning over the rail so I can get closer to his face, I look deep into his eyes. Beautiful, warm brown eyes of a man who just gets me in all ways. "It won't happen again. I won't run again unless it's into your arms, Bodie. I promise."

"Well, then," he says after a moment's pause. "I guess I love you, too."

My smile is immediate, and it's never been brighter. "Really?"

"I'd love you more if you'd move your hand down about twelve inches." His eyes are sparkling with mischief, but he wouldn't stop me if I did as he asked.

I consider for a moment, actually start to tug my hand out from under his, but then a nurse walks in. "Good morning, Mr. Wright," she says brightly.

Bodie groans and looks at me like someone just stole

his favorite toy or something.

The nurse walks around the opposite side of the bed and checks his IV line.

"Guess what, nurse?" Bodie says as his head rolls her way on the pillow.

"What's that?" she asks with a smile on her face but still working with the IV.

"My girl here just told me she loved me for the first time," he says, and my face flames hot. Bodie has never looked more boyish to me than he does now, grinning like a lunatic at the nurse.

"Oh, that's so sweet." The nurse looks charmed. I can tell she's a woman who loves a good romantic story.

"Think it's a good time for me to ask her to marry me?" he asks her.

Her head snaps to look at him with her jaw dropped wide, and I feel like someone just pumped a lightning bolt straight down my spine.

"Well, she is pregnant with my kid," Bodie explains to the nurse without even sparing me a glance. "And she says she loves me, so I'm thinking there's no reason not to."

The nurse gets her bearings and steps in closer to the bed. She leans over and lays a gentle hand on Bodie's shoulder. In a very pronounced whisper, as if she's giving him some secretive advice, but clearly loud enough for me to hear, she says, "I think, Mr. Wright, that perhaps you should wait until you have a pretty ring and you can get down on one knee. That's what every girl wants."

"Huh," Bodie says as he scratches his chin. His head rolls on the pillow, and he looks back to me. "That true?"

God, I love him.

I nod. "Kind of. I mean, if you're going to do it right and all."

"Noted," he says with a wink and then crooks his finger. "I would like to ask for a kiss, though. I think I'm long overdue one."

"Now that I can do," I tell him with a smile. "I really love you, Bodie. You know that, right?"

"I know it. Know it as deeply as I know I love you right back."

I lean over the rail, and Bodie lifts his head from the pillow. We meet in the middle, and his lips on mine are the perfect completion to how our story should end.

Well, not really…

EPILOGUE

Bodie

"**A**RE YOU NERVOUS?" I ask Rachel.

In truth, she looks relaxed as she sits on the edge of the exam table, legs crossed at the ankles while she swings them carelessly.

"Excited," she says in response to my question. "I totally want to do the nursery in an Iron Man theme, so as soon as Dr. Anchors confirms we're having a boy, I'm going to put a hurting on my credit card."

"God, you're the most adorable mom-to-be in the world," I say with a chuckle before leaning in to rub my cheek on her temple.

The door opens, and Dr. Anchors walks in. He's holding a folder in his hand, and I tense slightly. We have to get through the amnio results before we can get to the good stuff.

It's been a little over two weeks since the procedure.

A week since Rachel told me she loved me.

Life is good and will continue to be so, regardless of

what's in that folder. Rachel and I have spent a lot of time discussing "what ifs" this past week, and we're both of the mind that what will be will be.

Last night, Rachel said, "We can handle anything as long as we're together."

I pretty much attacked her after she said that. She does that a lot lately. Says things that catch me off guard and are very "un-Rachel-like". They make me fucking horny as hell. My busted elbow has done nothing to slow me down in that respect. I've just had to get creative, that's all.

"Rachel, Bodie," Dr. Anchors says lightly as he smiles at us. "I'm not going to beat around the bush. All testing from the amnio is fine. The baby doesn't have any detectable chromosomal abnormalities."

I let out a huge sigh of relief, and Rachel giggles nervously. Our hands reach out and clasp without even looking at each other.

"Let's get that ultrasound done, shall we?" Dr. Anchors says.

"Let's," Rachel agrees. She lays back on the examination table, dragging her t-shirt up to expose her belly. She doesn't even wait for Dr. Anchors, but also pushes down the waistband of the yoga pants to clear the path for the gel and wand.

Dr. Anchors chuckles as he adjusts the machine and pulls out the bottle of gel. I step in closer to the table, my hand taking Rachel's again.

I suck air into my lungs and hold it there. Impossibly hold it forever as Dr. Anchors squirts the cool liquid on Rachel's stomach, which is starting to round beautifully at seventeen weeks. She hisses slightly from the coldness, and then her hand squeezes mine as the wand starts gliding over her stomach.

An image appears on the screen... it looks like blobs to me at first, but—is that the head? I think it is. As the wand slowly moves, it becomes so clear what we're looking at. The wonder of it all overwhelms me. The 3D technology gives so much detail it's absolutely magical.

"There we go," Dr. Anchors murmurs as he moves the wand slowly and taps a few keys on the keyboards to take measurements. Then my heart practically explodes when he points to the screen. "Right there. You were right, Rachel... it's a boy."

"A boy," I whisper in awe as I look at Rachel.

"A boy," she says in an "I told you so" tone punctuated with a nod of her head.

Dr. Anchors marks two spots on the screen with the mouse. "Those are the little boy parts in between those two dots I just marked."

"Holy cow," I wheeze. "Is it me or is he already well endowed? A chip off the old block."

Rachel's hand slips from mine before popping me in the chest. I give an exaggerated *oomph* while Dr. Anchors laughs.

For the next ten minutes, Dr. Anchors records the

images and takes measurements. We ask him to focus time and time again on the face, which has amazing clarity given how little our kid is.

"He has your nose," I tell Rachel.

"Your smile," she says. I mean... you can even see the baby smile.

"I'd normally print a few of these off for you to take along with a DVD I'll give you, but this stupid printer isn't printing." As if to punctuate his frustration, he taps extra hard on a button on the small printer below the ultrasound machine. "I'm sorry. I'm going to get someone to come in and look at this. Why don't you get dressed and wait out in the lobby, and we'll get it figured out?"

"It's not a big deal," Rachel says lightly. "We can come back later."

"Of course it's a big deal," I scoff. I turn to Dr. Anchors. "Thanks. We'll just wait out in the lobby."

Dr. Anchors leaves to get a technician, and Rachel gets dressed. She chatters up a storm about the nursery and picking a name. We've already developed individual lists of names we like. I, of course, did a list for boys and girls. Rachel only did boys, convinced she was correct about the gender.

We sit out in the lobby, heads bent toward each other and whispering about baby shit. It's filled almost to capacity with pregnant women, some with their partners. I wonder if any of them are having as good a day as I am.

Rachel practically jumps in her seat she's so excited, and it almost threatens to unman me.

Seeing her like this.

She's come so far in such a brief time. My biggest joy was when she realized she wanted to be a mom, but her telling me she loves me was a close second. If all goes well, today's going to be fucking amazing, too.

"Miss Hart," the receptionist says from the front desk.

Rachel stands up and practically skips up to the front. I don't walk with her. Instead, I stay just a few feet behind her.

When she grabs the manila folder the receptionist hands her, I know she won't be able to resist tearing it open. Her fingers rip at the seal, and she reaches in like a kid reaching into their Halloween bucket to pull candy out.

She pulls a single sheet of paper out, turning it around to look at it, and I almost laugh when she gasps so loud several people in the waiting room turn to look at her.

I reach in my pocket and drop to one knee as Rachel slowly turns around to look at me.

You see, Dr. Anchors and I were cohorts today. His little act in the examination room telling us he couldn't print the 3D ultrasound pictures was really good.

Rachel's eyes are wide and blinking as she stares at me. The picture she'd pulled out of the envelope slips from her fingers and flutters to the ground. It lands face up right by my knee, a photograph of the engagement ring I'd bought the day after I got out of the hospital last week.

I pop the box open that holds the actual ring and hold it out to her. Her eyes flick down to the ring, and then back to me. "The nurse at the hospital said I should make it more romantic and put a little more thought into the engagement, so... here we go."

"Oh, Jesus," Rachel murmurs as her hand comes up to cover her mouth. I'm totally stoked when I see her eyes start to glisten with tears. A woman to my right sighs loudly in appreciation of my gesture, and the air crackles with electricity when I clear my throat.

"Rachel... this is not where I thought my life would take me. But I've always been a believer in accepting the gifts that are handed to me. And you are the greatest gift I've ever been given, our baby being the next greatest. The only thing that could ever be better is if you trust in what we have between us, and agree to share your life permanently with me while we raise our baby together. So, Rachel Hart... please, please... will you marry me?"

She doesn't make me suffer. In fact, she had started frantically nodding at about the time I talked about raising our baby together as husband and wife. Rachel drops to her knees and carefully slides her arms around my neck, so as not to bump into my elbow that I've got secured with a sling. I bobble the box but quickly secure it in my fist, pressing my cheek into hers.

"Is that a yes?" I ask, even though she's still nodding her head exuberantly.

"It's a yes," she says on a half sob, and everyone in the waiting room breaks out in applause.

Rachel presses her face into my neck, laughing with a mixture of embarrassment and delight. When she pulls back, she's shaking her head in bemusement. "I can't believe you did this."

"I've totally got romantic skills."

"You should have just asked in the hospital room," she says before pressing a quick kiss to my mouth. "I would have said yes then."

"But then you wouldn't have this cool story to tell our kid," I point out.

"Or have fodder for all the guys at Jameson to harass the shit out of you for," she returns with an evil sort of giggle.

"You're rotten," I tell her, holding the box out in front of her face. "But regardless, let's get this puppy on your finger and make it official."

Rachel holds her left hand out, and it trembles slightly. I'm dexterous enough to wrangle the ring from the box one handed, but I have to drop the black velvet carrier to the floor to do so.

The ring is beautiful. My mom helped me pick it out. She was thrilled that things worked out, far preferring me to be happy with a woman I love and the mother of my child than me moving back home to the farm. I expect I'll want my kid to be as happy one day, and will have to let them go.

The 3-carat yellow diamond slides on perfectly, and Rachel gets her first good look at it.

"Holy shit, Bodie," she gasps as she takes it in. "This is too much. I don't wear jewelry, you know."

"You wear this," I say emphatically, pulling her hand to my mouth where I kiss her knuckles. "Unless you're on a mission. Then it goes in a safe-deposit box."

Rachel laughs and nods. "Okay. I'll do that for you."

"That's my girl."

Again, her arms go around my neck. She presses into me carefully, ever aware of my injured arm. It sucks I can't crush her to me, but there will be time for that later.

We have, as a matter of fact, the rest of our lives.

"I love you," I whisper into her ear as we hug it out… on our knees in the lobby of Dr. Anchors' office while his patients watch.

"I love you, Bodie," she says, the quaver in her voice betraying just how emotional she is right now.

"Going to have a great life together."

"The best."

"Better than the best," I counter.

"Shut up and kiss me," she replies, and I give my girl what she wants.

Thank you for visiting The Wicked Horse! If you enjoyed reading *Wicked Choice* as much as I enjoyed writing it, please consider leaving a review.

The seduction continues at The Wicked Horse! Check out all the books available from *The Wicked Horse Vegas*. Each sexy novel can be read as a standalone.

Don't miss another new release by Sawyer Bennett!!! Sign up for her newsletter and keep up to date on new releases, giveaways, book reviews and so much more.
sawyerbennett.com/signup

Check out all the books available from Sawyer Bennett.
sawyerbennett.com/bookshop

Connect with Sawyer online:

Website: sawyerbennett.com

Twitter: www.twitter.com/bennettbooks

Facebook: www.facebook.com/bennettbooks

To see Other Works by Sawyer Bennett, please visit her Book Page on her website.

About the Author

Since the release of her debut contemporary romance novel, Off Sides, in January 2013, Sawyer Bennett has released multiple books, many of which have appeared on the New York Times, USA Today and Wall Street Journal bestseller lists.

A reformed trial lawyer from North Carolina, Sawyer uses real life experience to create relatable, sexy stories that appeal to a wide array of readers. From new adult to erotic contemporary romance, Sawyer writes something for just about everyone.

Sawyer likes her Bloody Marys strong, her martinis dirty, and her heroes a combination of the two. When not bringing fictional romance to life, Sawyer is a chauffeur, stylist, chef, maid, and personal assistant to a very active daughter, as well as full-time servant to her adorably naughty dogs. She believes in the good of others, and that a bad day can be cured with a great work-out, cake, or even better, both.

Sawyer also writes general and women's fiction under the pen name S. Bennett and sweet romance under the name Juliette Poe.

Made in the USA
Columbia, SC
04 January 2018